Southamp
Cruise Ship Christian
Bo

Hope Callaghan

hopecallaghan.com
Copyright © 2019
All rights reserved.

*****

**Visit my website for new releases and
special offers: hopecallaghan.com**

Acknowledgments

Thank you to these wonderful ladies who help make my books shine - Peggy H., Cindi G., Jean P., Wanda D., Barbara W., Renate P. and Alix C. for taking the time to preview *Southampton Stalker,* for the extra sets of eyes and for catching my mistakes.

Thank you to Sheila G. for making sure Millie's British Isles' Adventures are authentic.

A special THANKS to my reader review team:

Alice, Alta, Amary, Amy, Becky, Brenda, Carolyn, Charlene, Christine, Debbie, Denota, Devan, Diann, Grace, Helen, Jo-Ann, Jean M, Judith, Meg, Megan, Linda, Patsy, Polina, Rebecca, Rita, Theresa, Valerie and Virginia.

Contents

Cast of Characters

Mildred Sanders Armati. Mildred "Millie" Armati, heartbroken after her husband left her for one of his clients, decides to take a position as assistant cruise director aboard the mega cruise ship, Siren of the Seas. From day one, she discovers she has a knack for solving mysteries, which is a good thing since some sort of crime is always being committed on the high seas.

Annette Delacroix. Director of Food and Beverage on board Siren of the Seas, Annette has a secret past and is the perfect accomplice in Millie's investigations. Annette is the "Jill of all Trades" and isn't afraid to roll up her sleeves and help out her friend in need.

Catherine "Cat" Wellington. Cat is the most cautious of the group of friends and prefers to help Millie from the sidelines. But when push comes to shove, Cat can be counted on to risk life and limb in the pursuit of justice.

Three times I pleaded with the Lord to take it away from me. But he said to me, "My grace is sufficient for you, for my power is made perfect in weakness." Therefore, I will boast all the more gladly about my weaknesses, so that Christ's power may rest on me. That is why, for Christ's sake, I delight in weaknesses, in insults, in hardships, in persecutions, in difficulties. For when I am weak, then I am strong. Corinthians 12:8-10 (NIV)

Chapter 1

Danielle caught Millie's eye as she hurried across the crowded lounge. "What did I miss?"

"Nothing. Andy's waiting on someone to make the big announcement. For the life of me, I can't figure out what it is, and it's been driving me nuts."

Millie knew something was afoot when Andy started holing up inside his office. People came and went...Donovan Sweeney, the ship's purser, Dave Patterson, head of security, as well as Millie's husband, Captain Armati.

Despite her best attempts to wheedle even a tiny clue from her husband about what was going on, he was tight-lipped. In fact, every time she brought it up, he used the line - "Loose lips sink ships."

Which added to Millie's level of concern...Andy and surprises were rarely a good combination.

Danielle tapped the entertainment staff's scheduling watch strapped to her wrist. "Ack."

"What's wrong?"

"My scheduling app is on the fritz and keeps zapping me."

Someone nudged Millie's back, crowding her space. "It's time for me to move."

Danielle, noting the look of discomfort on her friend's face, placed a light hand under her elbow and blazed a path through the crowded room.

Annette, another of Millie's friends, slipped inside and met them in the back. "Any word?"

"Not yet. We're still waiting for someone."

Donovan Sweeney appeared in the doorway. He circled the crowd before joining Andy on stage. They shook hands, and Donovan whispered something in Andy's ear before reaching for the microphone.

The purser's surprise appearance caused a hush to fall over the room's occupants. "Thank you for joining us this morning. First of all, I would like to thank you, the entertainment staff, for doing such a fantastic job of keeping our passengers happy during our Transatlantic crossing."

Donovan continued. "I spoke with Captain Armati. The ship is making excellent time. We'll be arriving in Southampton ahead of schedule and docking by six o'clock this evening."

Millie had already heard from her husband that the ship was ahead of schedule. They'd cleared the early arrival with the port authorities, and although she had enjoyed the crossing, she was looking forward to planting her feet on dry land again.

Siren of the Seas would be in the Southampton port for a couple of days before the next set of passengers boarded the ship for their first twelve-day British Isles cruise.

The ship's first stop would be Saint Peter Port / Guernsey. Millie was scheduled to work the entire day. She was disappointed until she learned she would have time off the following day which was when she planned to visit Blarney Castle near Cork, Ireland.

She still hadn't lined up anyone to go with her, although she knew it wouldn't be Nic. He wouldn't be leaving the ship or taking time off for the first full twelve-day cruise and depending on how it went, possibly not even the second.

There was a murmur in the crowd at Donovan's announcement, and Millie briefly wondered if this was Andy's surprise. Based on his broad grin, she had a feeling the early arrival announcement was only the tip of the iceberg.

"Our passengers aren't scheduled to disembark until tomorrow morning. We're giving them the option to disembark ahead of time but believe most will remain on board or leave the ship and then return for the night." Donovan droned on about making sure the passengers' experience was top notch. "Depending on your work schedule, once we clear customs, those of you with free time will be allowed to get off the ship."

There was a round of spontaneous applause, and Donovan waited for the crowd to quiet down. "I know Andy appreciates all of your hard work, as well, and we hope you enjoy our time in the British Isles. And now, I would like to make a special announcement." He motioned to someone standing off stage and behind the curtains.

All eyes turned as Isla Peterson, another of Millie's friends and someone who regularly filled in for Millie and Danielle when they needed an extra hand, emerged.

Isla smiled nervously as she slowly made her way across the stage.

"Isla joined Siren of the Seas last year. Many of you know and have worked with her. She's been a wonderful addition to the entertainment staff. Our current director of shore excursions has decided to pursue a career in the UK and will be leaving us tonight. Isla, who has previous experience as a travel agent in the States, has accepted the position."

Millie was the first one to burst into a round of applause, and the rest of the crew joined in. Isla's nervous smile disappeared as Andy handed her a crisp jacket, the ones worn by the ship's directors.

She slipped it on, and then Donovan handed her the microphone. "Thank you, everyone. I...I have some big shoes to fill, and I'm thrilled to know I'll still be working with all of you in the entertainment department, just in a different capacity." Isla quickly handed the microphone back to him and hurried off the stage.

Donovan thanked them again for their hard work during the Transatlantic crossing and dismissed the crowd. Millie watched in disbelief as he exited the stage. "That's all? I mean, not that I'm not thrilled for Isla, although there's no way I would take the position since you have to go on all of those crazy shore excursions as part of your job."

"I would do it," Danielle said. "Isla lucked out. I had no idea she worked in the travel industry. That's cool about time off this evening. Are you going to head out?"

Millie shrugged. Andy was hosting the Fond Farewell show. After that was Blackjack Blaze's final SeaFi show. She'd planned to clean the apartment and hang around home before doing her rounds for the late evening entertainment, but the prospect of getting off the ship, even if it was only for a short amount of time, was tempting.

"I'll go with you," Danielle offered. "Maybe this was part of Andy's surprise...to give us a couple of hours off."

"Yeah." Millie warmed to the idea. "Maybe we should have a look around. I've done some research, and the ship's dock is within walking distance to some shops and restaurants."

The room cleared except for Andy and a couple of the other crewmembers. "I want to have a word with Andy before I leave."

"Because you think this isn't all of the surprises," Danielle guessed.

"Exactly. I think there's more." Millie waited for the crewmembers to leave before approaching the stage.

"Well?" Andy beamed. "Are you going to get off the ship and have a look around?"

"Yeah, but that's not all," Millie said bluntly. "I'm thrilled for Isla. I think she'll be a good fit for director of shore excursions, but there's something else."

"What makes you think that?"

"Because we know you," Danielle chimed in.

"You're right." Andy straightened, giving the women his full attention. "There is another surprise, but I would rather show you and not tell you."

Millie sucked in a breath and briefly closed her eyes, suspecting there was a good reason for her concern. "When do you plan to show us?"

Andy consulted his watch. "In a couple of hours." He tapped the top eyeing them thoughtfully. "Meet me in my office at six, as soon as the ship docks. It won't take long."

"Both of us?" Danielle asked.

"Yes, both of you." Another crewmember returned to the stage to ask about time off, and Danielle and Millie exited the lounge.

Millie waited until they were in the hall to talk. "What do you think?"

"That we're in trouble," Danielle joked.

Chapter 2

There was a buzz in the air after Andy's ship-wide announcement about docking early, giving passengers the option to disembark or stay on board until the following morning.

Millie fielded an array of questions. The most popular ones concerned a curfew for those who planned to explore the port and return to the ship. It took a few back and forth calls between Donovan, Andy and Millie's husband, Nic, to get the final word that once the ship cleared customs, there was a mandatory midnight all aboard to make sure passengers were back in time to pack their belongings and exit a final time the following morning.

Millie hustled to the crew cafeteria to grab a tossed salad and a bowl of soup before hosting a round of trivia about the British Isles. Her excitement grew as the afternoon wore on, and when she passed by an empty window seat, she slowed long enough to check the ship's position.

The passengers began heading outdoors and lining the railings, a sign they were getting close. She joined them on an open deck and could see land on both sides as a small pilot boat pulled alongside the ship, preparing for the harbor pilot to board and finish guiding them to their berth.

Despite her excitement and the distraction, the show had to go on. She cast the shoreline a wistful glance and made her way to the miniature golf course for a final goofy golf competition. Up next was an art-themed scavenger hunt, followed by a speed painting class in the atrium.

It was during the speed painting when Millie felt the ship shudder as the thrusters engaged, and the ship began making its way to the docking area.

The speed painting was Millie's favorite event of the day. There were three unique options to choose from...a landscape of native flowers, Guernsey

"A local who also happens to be a good friend." Andy's radio started to squawk. It was Suharto. "Andy...do you copy?"

"Right on time." Andy snatched the radio off the table. "Go ahead, Suharto."

"You're needed down at the gangway."

"I'm on my way." Andy scrambled out of the chair and strode to the door. "Don't move. I'll be right back."

Millie watched him leave. "Andy hired a friend, a local expert. I guess it makes sense. Isla is going to need some time to get up to speed and learn her new job."

"Yeah. So maybe this person is taking Isla's spot while we're here."

"I wonder why Andy didn't mention it before," Millie murmured. Andy loved surprises. Sometimes they were good while others...not so good. Hopefully, this was the former.

The women chatted about their upcoming schedules until they heard Andy's heavy footsteps crossing the backstage. Andy appeared first, and his "surprise" trailed behind. It was a medium-build woman with bright red hair, her ringlet curls springing up all over her head. She and Andy laughed about something as they entered the room.

"Millie...Danielle." Andy cleared his throat. "I would like you to meet my old friend, Sophia Williams. As I mentioned earlier, Sophia is an expert on the British Isles. She'll be working with us for the summer season."

Millie slipped out of her chair. She extended her hand, a smile on her face. Sophia smiled back, but there was something about her expression that sent a cold chill down Millie's spine. "It's nice to meet you, Sophia."

"Millie is Captain Armati's wife," Andy explained.

"Ah." Sophia lifted a brow, eyeing Millie with interest. "I should be mindful to be on my best behavior."

Millie released her grip, and Danielle and Sophia greeted each other. "We're moving Sophia into Blackjack's cabin after he leaves tomorrow." Andy turned to Sophia, a concerned look on his face. "Do you have accommodations for this evening?"

"I'm staying at the Falcon Tavern. It's a short walk from here." Sophia let out a husky laugh. "I can always check out and bunk with you, Andrew."

Andy's face turned a bright red. He shot Millie a quick look. "Yes. Uh. I would offer you my cabin, but it's small." He changed the subject, giving Sophia a brief overview of the ship and Isla's duties.

Millie could see Sophia had completely tuned him out, and she could also tell from the look on her face that the wheels were spinning in her mind. For the second time, the woman's arrival filled her with an uneasiness.

"Andrew?" Millie teased.

"Sophia has always called me Andrew. I go by Andy while working since it's less formal and more casual." Andy wrapped up his speech and then offered to give Sophia a tour, which she immediately accepted.

"Can we visit the bridge? I would *love* to meet the captain." Sophia nearly purred, and Millie instinctively clenched her fists. The longer she was around the woman, the less she liked her.

"We'll let you two start the tour." Millie grabbed Danielle's hand and pulled her to the office door. "Danielle and I will be back around nine, in plenty of time to start our night shifts." The women exited the office, and the tinkle of Sophia's laughter followed them.

Millie stopped when they reached the theater's exit. "Well? First impressions."

Danielle blew air through thinned lips. "You better keep an eye on your hubby. That woman is on the prowl."

"I was thinking the same thing." Millie grimaced. "I don't get a good feeling about her. Andy seems smitten."

"Smitten?" Danielle snorted. "I thought he was going to hand her his all-access keycard, not to mention give her his cabin."

"Or let her move in with him," Millie muttered. "Maybe we're way off, and Sophia just isn't good with first impressions."

"Let's hope. You about ready to head out?"

"Yeah. I told Cat we would meet her outside the gangway at six-thirty. I want to run upstairs to check on Scout and then I'll meet both of you there."

"Sounds good." Danielle gave her friend a thumbs up and strode to the crewmembers only doorway while Millie headed upstairs to the bridge.

Not only was Nic on the bridge, but Staff Captain Antonio Vitale and a man Millie guessed was the harbor pilot were there as well. They were studying the navigational board and didn't notice her as she quietly made her way down the hall to the apartment.

Scout, their teacup Yorkie, was waiting at the door. Millie scooped him up and held him close. "Sorry that I couldn't make it back earlier." She carried him to the balcony and stepped outside.

The ship was anchored, and several stevedores buzzed back and forth on their forklifts. The docking area was calm compared to typical turnover days when the crew was offloading trash and passenger's luggage and then onloading provisions along with the next group's luggage.

Since the ship was early, Millie guessed they wouldn't be busy until the following morning. Millie tossed the ball to Scout a couple of times and then ran upstairs to change her clothes. There was a nip in the early evening air, so on her way out, she grabbed a jacket and shoved it into her backpack.

By the time Millie returned to the bridge, the harbor pilot was gone, and only Nic and Antonio remained. Nic caught his wife's eye and made his way over. "Andy was here a few minutes ago. He said you and Danielle were going to have a look around the port."

"We are." Millie patted her backpack. "Do you mind?"

"Of course not. I wish I could go with you. Maybe next time."

"Or the time after that," Millie joked. "Did you meet the British Isles resident expert, Sophia?"

"I did."

"And?"

"And what?" Nic asked.

"What did you think of her?"

"I trust Andy's judgment. He was wise in choosing someone local to assist passengers in exploring the ports."

Millie made an unhappy noise, and Nic lifted a brow. "What is it?"

His wife glanced over her husband's shoulder at the staff captain and lowered her voice. "There's something about her."

"You don't like her, yet you just met her."

"It's not that I don't like her. She gave off a weird vibe and was a little overly-anxious to meet you."

"Ah." Nic nodded knowingly. "You think she's interested in me."

"Let's just say Sophia is worth keeping an eye on."

Nic chuckled. "And you're the self-appointed watcher."

"Of course." Millie shifted her backpack to her other shoulder. "I better get going. I'll be back around nine to change and start my shift."

"Be careful," Nic warned. "It's an unfamiliar port. Be on your guard and mindful of your surroundings."

Millie bounced on her tiptoes and gave her husband a peck on the cheek. "I will. Cat is going with us, too."

When she reached the gangway, Cat and Danielle were already waiting. It was a short walk from the exit, along the pier and onto the main thoroughfare. There was a small park directly across the street.

"I need to bring Scout here," Millie said. "He would love this."

After touring the park, they strolled to a more populated area, this one lined with shops and pubs with a hotel on the corner.

"Falcon Tavern," Millie read the name. "Isn't this the name of the place where Sophia is staying tonight?"

"Yeah. There's a pub down below." Danielle peered at the sidewalk's display board and the daily specials. "Fish and chips. We have to try fish and chips."

"Yes, we do."

The trio sauntered past the shopping area, stopping at several gift shops to look around.

They found a small variety store a block farther from the ship where the women stocked up on necessities. It took Millie a moment to calculate the conversion between dollars and pounds.

"We should start back," Danielle said.

After paying for their purchases, the trio cut through the center of the small park and began crossing the street when Cat abruptly stopped. "I can't believe it."

"Can't believe what?" Millie asked.

"Over there." Cat excitedly pointed to the busy intersection.

"What am I looking at?" Millie squinted her eyes.

"It's a British telephone box. I hoped there was one around here somewhere." Cat tugged on Millie's arm, dragging her down the sidewalk while Danielle jogged alongside trying to keep up.

When they reached the red telephone box, Cat released her grip on Millie's arm. "I've done some research on these. If I'm not mistaken, this is a kiosk two, nicknamed the 'K2.' There were several more versions created over the years, but this one is the most well-known."

Cat slowly circled the box. "The red phone boxes were at risk of disappearing altogether until an 'Adopt a Kiosk' program began, making the communities responsible for their upkeep. There are only about eleven thousand left."

Cat pulled her cell phone from her jacket pocket, switched it on and snapped a picture. "I was hoping I would get to see one, and can you believe we found it on the first day?" She took a second picture and began waving at Millie and Danielle. "Get inside so I can take your picture."

Millie wrinkled her nose, warily eyeing the cramped interior. "It's too small."

"There's plenty of room in there. Please?"

"All right." Millie reluctantly crossed the sidewalk. "You too, Danielle."

Danielle followed Millie inside. "Gross. What is that awful smell?"

Millie pinched the end of her nose. "Decades of body odor?"

"It's making me sick." Danielle pointed at Cat. "Hurry up. This thing is smelly."

A woman approached, attempting to ease past Cat, and she stopped her. "Excuse me. Would you mind taking our picture?"

"I would be delighted."

"Thanks." Cat handed the woman her phone and darted into the box, squeezing in front of Millie, whose back was now pressed against the rear glass panels. She began to feel lightheaded and sucked in a quick breath.

"This is so much fun," Cat clapped her hands.

Danielle, noting Millie's discomfort, started to reply. "I don't think..."

The woman snapped the picture and handed Cat her phone back. "Thanks again." She waited for the woman to walk away. "I wonder if the door actually shuts." Cat began closing the door.

"Cat..." Millie gasped. "I can't breathe."

"What?" Cat attempted to turn toward Millie, brushing her backside against the partially closed door and forcing it shut. *Clunk.*

"Millie's claustrophobia," Danielle said. "We gotta get out of here."

Cat fumbled with the handle, frantically trying to open the door. "I...I can't find the latch."

"Let me try." Danielle and Cat shifted at the same time, eliminating Millie's last bit of space and wedging her hips between a narrow metal shelf and the phone box.

"Please hurry." The room began to spin, and Millie closed her eyes, praying that they would find a way to get the door open.

"The door is stuck."

Chapter 3

Danielle braced her arms and pushed against the frame. "Hang on, Millie." She placed both hands at the top and pressed hard as she gently tapped the bottom of the door with the tip of her sneaker. "It won't budge."

"It looks like there's a branch wedged under the bottom," Cat said.

Danielle tried again, pressing on the top of the door frame as she kicked the bottom.

"Let me help." Cat began kicking the heel of her shoe.

Millie pressed her palm against the cool, glass panel. "We may have to break the glass."

"Break the glass?" Cat stopped kicking and eyed Millie in disbelief. "This is a historic national icon."

"Not to mention that we could probably end up getting arrested for damaging city property." Danielle grunted again, and the top of the door wobbled. "I think I've almost got it."

The door swung open, and the women scrambled out.

Millie bent down, placing both hands on her knees as she closed her eyes and sucked in a breath of fresh air. "Thank you, God."

"I'm sorry, Millie," Cat apologized. "I got so excited about the phone box, I forgot all about your claustrophobia."

"It's okay." Millie could feel her pulse begin to slow, and she straightened her back. "That's one for the books...being trapped inside a phone booth."

"Did you see the old phone inside?" Cat asked excitedly.

"Not only did I see it, I'm pretty sure the outline of the receiver is imprinted on my back," Millie joked.

"I want to get a few more pictures." Cat darted back inside for a few moments before joining Danielle and Millie. "This was so awesome. I can't believe we actually found one of these."

The women reached the corner and waited for the light to change before crossing the street that ran alongside the terminal. "Check out the tall ship. It looks old."

The women made a detour for a closer inspection of the antique sailing ship, which appeared to be in the midst of extensive renovations. "I bet the interior of this baby is pretty awesome," Danielle said admiringly. "I wouldn't mind taking a tour."

"You're on your own," Millie said. "All I can envision is dark, cramped spaces with little to no air."

Danielle chuckled. "Cat, I think you've traumatized Millie."

"I'm fine." Millie cast an anxious eye at the darkening skies. "We should keep moving."

"You're right."

The women had wandered into what appeared to be an industrial area. A long metal fence lined the right-hand side. Several warehouses were on the other side of the fence, the same ones Millie had noticed earlier from her apartment's balcony.

They picked up the pace and started to pass by. The first was shuttered for the evening. The one next to it appeared abandoned and had chunks of broken glass protruding from the rectangular windows.

The warehouse's small service door was wide open with bags of trash piled next to the door and spilling onto the sidewalk. There was a dull *thud* coming from inside the warehouse followed by a shuffling sound.

Millie shivered involuntarily, filled with the distinct feeling they were being watched. "We need to get a move on," she whispered urgently, regretting the fact they had let time get away from them.

"Yes, we do." Danielle must've felt the same.

Straight ahead was Siren of the Seas. The women had almost cleared the buildings when a man emerged from the shadows, blocking their path, a shiny object glinting in his hand.

Chapter 4

Millie instinctively reached for her backpack containing her cell phone, her purse and her ship's identification.

Danielle, sensing a potentially dangerous situation, leaped into action and stepped in front of her friends.

The man took a menacing step toward them, beaming a flashlight in Millie's face. "Don't you know it's not safe hanging around here at night?"

"We're crewmembers on board Siren of the Seas," Millie said. "We're new to the area and just arrived in port."

"I figured as much. You shouldn't be out here after dark. It's not safe," he repeated.

Millie shifted to the left, attempting to sidestep the man. "Thank you for the warning."

The man swayed slightly as he leaned in. Millie could smell alcohol on his breath, and he reeked of stale cigarettes.

"Can you spare a coupla quid for an old man?"

"A quid?" Millie's eyes widened.

Danielle patted her pockets. "We don't have any British pounds or currency."

"American dollars work the same." The man extended a hand while Cat fumbled inside her jacket pocket. She handed him a five-dollar bill. "This is all I have."

The man crumpled the bill in his hand, eyeing Millie, who was closest. "I might have a dollar or two." She unzipped her backpack and stuck her hand inside. The tips of her fingers touched a small bundle of bills. She thrust three ones in his outstretched palm. "We really need to be going."

"Thank you for the kindness." He gave the women a toothless grin and began backing away. "Remember what I said."

"We will." Danielle propelled Cat and Millie forward. They took off at a dead run toward the ship. The women didn't slow until they reached the security checkpoint.

The guard manning the gate stepped forward. "Is everything okay?"

"I...yes. We're fine." Millie struggled to catch her breath as she fumbled for her picture ID. "We were walking through the port when a homeless guy stopped us."

"You may want to give anyone leaving the ship a heads up to avoid the area over there," Cat motioned in the direction they'd just come from.

"Over where?" The man craned his neck.

"To the left and near the abandoned building," Danielle said.

"I'll send a foot patrol to check it out."

Millie passed through the gate. "We need to tell Andy and Dave Patterson what happened. They might want to issue an advisory to the crew and passengers."

"He seemed pretty harmless," Danielle said. "Although he did scare us half to death."

The women climbed the crew gangway, swiping their keycards as they boarded the ship. "Andy has me working the singles final farewell. I better get going."

After Danielle left, Millie and Cat made a beeline for the security office. Patterson wasn't in, but Oscar, Patterson's second in command, was working.

The women briefly shared what had happened. Looking back, Millie was certain the man was a harmless vagrant. "I think he was harmless. He wanted a few bucks and to warn us."

"Nonetheless, it is good you decided to report it." Oscar assured them he would pass the information on to his boss, and they left.

Cat and Millie parted ways in the stairwell, with Millie returning home, through the bridge and into the apartment where she found Nic and Scout on the balcony.

"I'm back." Millie shrugged off her backpack. She dropped it on the dining room table and joined them outdoors.

"Finally. I was beginning to worry." Nic cast his wife a look of concern.

"The time got away from us."

"Did you get my text? I was getting ready to dispatch a search party."

"No. You sent me a message?" Millie returned to her backpack and retrieved her cell phone. There was a text from Nic, asking her to call him. "I'm sorry. I missed it."

"At least you're all right," Nic's expression relaxed. "You shouldn't be wandering around after dark in an area you're not familiar with."

Millie was on the fence about telling him about the vagrant incident but knew he would find out soon enough once he talked to Patterson and quickly decided she should be the one to tell him. "We were on our way back to the ship when we took a detour to check out the other end of the port area, not paying attention to the fact it was already getting dark."

She twined her fingers together, bracing for Nic's reaction. "A homeless man stopped us and asked us for cash."

"What?" Nic exploded. "Did he threaten you?"

"No." Millie hurried on, telling him the man had scared them when he stepped out of the dark warehouse. "He warned us to be careful. It won't happen again."

"You should know better than to wander around dark dock areas alone, especially women who are in a strange country. It could've been so much worse."

Millie nodded. She couldn't disagree with her husband. It had been foolish, but they hadn't planned on exploring that area of the port. "I'm sorry for scaring you."

"I'm sorry for getting upset. I was worried sick," Nic said as he rubbed the back of his neck. "We need to report the incident to Patterson so he can issue an advisory to the passengers."

"Cat and I already did. We told Oscar what happened." Millie slipped an arm around her husband's waist. "I think you need to punish me severely," she flirted.

Nic's expression softened. "I think you're right. I like the idea...a lot." He slowly lowered his head, kissing her gently.

Millie leaned in, all thoughts of creepy, dark warehouses and the homeless man far away.

Her scheduler app buzzed, and Millie jerked back. "Andy has impeccable timing."

Nic chuckled. "Yes, he does. My break is over anyway. It's time for me to return to the bridge."

Millie gave her husband a quick kiss before coaxing Scout inside. She waited for him to leave and then ran upstairs to change back into her work uniform.

While she dressed, she prayed for the poor man, wondering if he lived in the abandoned warehouse. Andy's message via the zap app requested Millie's presence in his office before beginning her evening rounds.

When she got there, she found Andy and Sophia Williams inside. They sat next to each other, with their heads close together.

Millie cleared her throat, and Andy's head shot up. She could've sworn Sophia had her hand on Andy's leg as she leaned back in the chair. "Millie. Thanks for coming down here so quickly."

"You're welcome."

"How was Southampton?"

"Eventful. What's up?"

"I found a spot for Sophia to hang her hat for the night, and she offered to start training with you this evening."

Millie's heart sank. "Training with me?"

"Yes. I'll be busy with the Fond Farewell show as well as the gala diamond party. I figured you could give Sophia a behind-the-scenes look at how the entertainment department runs."

A slow smile spread across Sophia's face or more like an evil grin.

"I...yes, of course." Millie tugged on the bottom of her jacket. "Are you planning on having her host events?"

"Perhaps to fill in. Sophia's main job will be to share her expertise with passengers by hosting lectures before each port stop." Andy consulted his watch. "It's almost showtime. I'll let you ladies get going."

Sophia eased out of the chair and joined Millie, who was still standing by the doorway. "I told Andrew he better not make this job too tempting, or I might be persuaded to stay and head back to the States with you."

"You'll have to see for yourself. It's full-time non-stop." Millie led the way out of Andy's office. "First up, we're hosting a jackpot bingo finale in the Marseille Lounge. After that, we'll check on Blackjack Blaze's SeaFi show. Later, we're in charge of hosting a round of Killer Karaoke."

They exited the theater, passing by passengers who were on their way in to snag a front row seat.

"Does the theater fill up for the shows?"

"Every night," Millie held the door for Sophia. "The Fond Farewell show is popular. Andy likes to surprise passengers with last minute giveaways. He'll hand out gift cards to the gift shops, discount coupons for upcoming cruises and specialty coffee shop vouchers."

"You like him?" Sophia asked.

"Him, who?"

"Andrew...do you like working for Andrew?"

"Yes. He's a great boss. Andy is very good at what he does, which is to keep the passengers entertained and engaged."

Sophia headed to a bank of elevators.

"I don't do elevators," Millie reached out to stop her.

"Huh?"

"I never take the elevators."

Sophia's jaw dropped. "So that's your secret for staying slim and trim."

"It's part of the reason." Millie began walking to the stairwell. "The assistant cruise director job keeps me on my toes."

The women climbed the stairs to deck nine. By the time they reached the upper deck, Sophia was out of breath, her face the same shade of red as her hair.

"I'm sorry," Millie apologized. "You can take the elevators and meet me."

"No." Sophia gasped. "I'll stick with you."

They arrived to find the lounge was already filling, and the women approached the stage.

After some brief instructions for Sophia, they began bingo promptly at ten, followed by bonus bingo and then a final bingo. The grand prize was cash and not a free cruise.

The passengers filed out, and Sophia plopped down in an empty chair while Millie stored the supplies. She wiggled her feet in the air as she eyed Millie. "I'm tired already."

"We have several more events to host."

Sophia kicked one of her shoes off and began rubbing her ankle. "I don't think I'm cut out to be a full-time entertainer."

Millie placed the bingo cage inside the cabinet and locked it. "It's not a job for everyone."

"Or anyone." Sophia wiggled her foot back into her shoe. "I met your husband earlier."

There was a pause, and Millie suspected Sophia was waiting for a reaction. Finally, the woman spoke. "How did you meet?"

"On board Siren of the Seas."

"No, I mean, out of all of the women on board this ship, how did you manage to catch the captain's eye?" Sophia asked bluntly.

"Let's just say I've had my share of adventures since joining Siren of the Seas, which put me on Nic's radar and not always in a positive way." Millie stepped off the stage. "It's time for us to hustle downstairs and check on the SeaFi show."

The rest of the evening passed quickly as the women moved from event-to-event. At one point, Millie was certain Sophia was ready to call it quits, but to her credit, she hung in there.

Millie wrapped up the final karaoke song and began placing the supplies in the cabinet. "We're done."

"Done?"

"You're free for the rest of the evening."

"Rest of what evening? I'm exhausted."

"It's a lot of hustling. I'll see you tomorrow." As Millie watched Sophia limp to the crew-only exit, her stomach began grumbling. She realized she hadn't eaten since Cat, Danielle and she had stopped by a sub shop to sample a local dish where the man behind the counter suggested the bacon sarnie - the British version of a sub sandwich.

Millie could almost feel her arteries harden when she discovered the traditional sandwich, consisting of two slices of soft, white bread, was filled with several layers of bacon and sliced tomatoes. She watched as the man coated the insides of the bread with a thick layer of softened butter. When he handed the plate to Millie, she could see butter oozing out both sides.

It was tasty, but the abundance of butter was too much, and she couldn't finish the sandwich. Danielle, on the other hand, devoured hers, ordered a second and inhaled both.

With limited food choices since most restaurants had closed, Millie settled on a slice of pepperoni pizza from the pizza station. She found a quiet table in the corner and gobbled the food, eating all of it except for the crunchy crust before trudging back to the apartment.

While she walked, she made a mental note to check on Annette, who had a doctor's appointment in Southampton the next day. She also thought about Sharky, the ship's head of maintenance, and his blind date with the Russian woman.

Despite her repeated attempts to convince Sharky to have someone go with him when he met the woman, so far, he had refused.

Not ready to give up, she planned to swing by his office the following morning after the Transatlantic passengers disembarked to try to talk some sense into him.

Millie was on her way home when her radio began to blare. "Charlie! Charlie! Charlie! Medical needed at the crew gangway."

Chapter 5

Millie's first thought was Cat, who was spending her evening helping the security staff screen the returning passengers and crewmembers. She changed direction and scrambled down the steps to the gangway.

Cat was nowhere in sight.

She hit the deck running, passing several other crewmembers who were headed in the same direction. When Millie arrived, she found a crowd had already gathered. Doctor Gundervan knelt near the entrance and next to a crewmember who was lying on the floor.

The only thing visible was a pair of black sneakers, standard shoes that were worn by all crewmembers. She inched forward, craning her neck in a desperate attempt to see who it was.

Millie finally got close enough, and her heart plummeted. It was Nikki Tan, one of the crewmembers who worked in guest services. There was a splotch of blood on her pale pink blouse and a cut on her lower lip. Two of the security staff wheeled a gurney down the long hallway. The onlookers shifted to the side, making room for the emergency crew.

The men gently loaded Nikki onto the stretcher and began wheeling her to the elevator. Dave Patterson was on hand, a serious expression on his face as he talked to the security guards near the gangway.

Cat was there too, her face pale and her hand trembling as she motioned toward the corridor.

Millie lingered behind, anxious to find out what had happened to Nikki. Her first thought was the beggar who had stopped them near the abandoned warehouse. Had he cornered Nikki while she was alone and attacked her?

Perhaps there was more than one person, and they had ganged up on the unsuspecting woman. She began to pray that Nikki's injuries weren't serious.

Finally, Patterson stepped away to have a private word with Oscar. He gave Oscar a curt nod and turned on his heel, which is when he caught Millie's eye and made his way over. "You saved me a trip."

"Saved you a trip?"

"You and Cat stopped by my office earlier. You told Oscar a man confronted you and asked for money."

"He did." Millie briefly repeated the story. "I'm sure both Oscar and Cat also told you what happened."

"They did. And now Nikki has been attacked."

Millie pressed a hand to her chest. "Was she alone?"

"Unfortunately, yes. A man and a woman dragged Nikki inside the building where they attacked and robbed her."

"That's awful."

"She started screaming for help. Our patrol guys heard her scream. By the time they got to her, the robbers were long gone, and Nikki was on the ground."

"Was the man an older man?"

"Unfortunately, we're not sure. I have my men searching the area, although I don't hold out much hope of finding them." Patterson sighed heavily. "A note is already being sent to each of the passengers' cabins, notifying them of the incidents and warning them to be careful."

Patterson's radio blared, and he excused himself. After he left, Millie wandered over to the gangway where Cat stood next to the checkpoint.

"Poor Nikki," Cat said.

"Patterson said Nikki's attackers were a man and woman. I'm not convinced the old man who stopped us is one of them."

"You never know. Maybe one of his friends showed up, and they ramped up their strategy to rob crewmembers."

"I suppose it's possible, but where was the second person - the woman - when we were stopped earlier? I mean, it's only been a few hours."

"I don't know," Cat shrugged. "All I know is I'm not going anywhere near the area again, especially after dark."

Millie chatted with her friend for a few more minutes before making her way upstairs to the bridge. Nic was nowhere in sight. One of the other captains and crewmembers were on the bridge, and Millie waved as she passed by.

The apartment was empty except for Scout, who was waiting by the door. She scooped him up and wandered onto the balcony. The dock area was crawling with ship's security, and Millie knew they were still searching for Nikki's attackers.

The door to the apartment slammed shut. "I'm home."

Millie stepped inside to find Nic kicking off his shoes. "I just left Donovan Sweeney's office after a briefing on tonight's attack."

"Poor Nikki." Millie set Scout on the floor. "I heard the emergency call for the crew gangway and ran down there. I haven't heard anything about her condition."

"She's staying in medical overnight for observation." Nic unbuttoned his jacket and hung it on the hook near the door. "I know we already discussed this, but I'm going to repeat that you are not to be wandering around this port alone after dark."

"I won't," Millie promised. "I'm not convinced the man who stopped Cat, Danielle and me earlier was one of Nikki's attackers." She remembered the man's warning before he asked them for money and repeated what he'd said to her husband. "I don't think it was him."

"Whether it was him or not makes little difference." Nic droned on about safety, about Millie not taking chances and staying close to the ship. "And last, but not least, no investigating."

"Me?" Millie's eyes widened innocently.

"Yes, you." Nic wagged his finger at his wife. "You heard me."

"Loud and clear." Millie stifled a yawn. "It's been a long day. I have to be up early to meet Andy at the gangway to see the passengers off." She trailed behind her husband and began following him up the stairs. She stopped midway and pointed at her latest creation. "What do you think?"

"About what?"

"This." Millie tapped the edge of the wooden frame. "I painted this today."

"It's lovely." Nic studied the painting. "What is it?"

"Niccolo Armati," Millie scolded. "It's a flower - the Tudor rose to be exact. It's England's national flower."

"Ah." He lifted a brow. "I see it now. It's very nice." Nic continued up the steps.

"You don't like it."

"You're right. I don't like it...I love it." They reached the top of the stairs, and he turned, pulling her into his arms. "The painting is beautiful, just like you."

"Nice try." Millie leaned into him. "I think I am getting better, though."

"So maybe you should focus on your artistic endeavors instead of your snooping endeavors."

Millie frowned. "When's the last time I stuck my nose in where it didn't belong?"

Nic chuckled.

"I'm serious." Millie followed him to the bathroom door. "I think I've been behaving myself."

"What about the woman who went overboard recently?"

"That doesn't count. Amit was on the hook for her death and..." Millie paused. "Besides, if you remember correctly, I helped track down her killer."

"This is an argument I most certainly won't win." Nic gave his wife a peck on the cheek and slipped into the bathroom.

"Hmm." Millie kicked her shoes off and tossed them into the closet. The look of aggravation was still on her face when Nic emerged a short time later. "Sharky is going on his blind date with the Russian woman tomorrow."

"Are you going with him?"

She shook her head. "He's going alone."

"He's a grown man." Nic pulled the covers back and climbed into bed. "You're a good friend, Millie, and a wonderful wife, but sometimes you need to butt out."

Millie mumbled something unintelligible under her breath and marched into the bathroom. She quickly calmed, realizing Nic was right. There were times she had to admit she probably overstepped boundaries, but it was mostly out of concern for family and friends.

She exited the bathroom, and Nic's eyes followed her as she crossed the room. "You're cute, even when you're cranky," he teased.

Millie waited for Scout to circle his small pillow. "I can see your point. Maybe I am a little gung ho at times."

"But only because you care." Nic placed a light hand on his wife's cheek and gently kissed her lips before pulling back. "And that's what I love about you. You're genuine, and you care."

He rolled over onto his pillow. "So, does this mean you're not going to start snooping around?"

"No. I'm not going to investigate. It could be an isolated incident." Millie shut off the bedside lamp before they clasped hands. The couple prayed for a safe summer, safety for the staff, the crewmembers and the passengers.

Millie squeezed his hand and released her grip. "I love you."

"I love you too; for the rest of my life."

Despite Millie's insistence she was going to keep her nose out of Nikki's attack, she couldn't help but wonder if she was wrong and the man who'd confronted them was the same one who had attacked her.

Her gut told her it wasn't, but there was no denying the evidence. The incident happened in nearly the same location and only a short time later. Before falling asleep, Millie prayed the security guards would apprehend the culprits.

*****

Millie's first stop the next morning was the ship's galley. She found her friend, Annette, already busy working. "You're up early."

"I have to be down at the gangway in a few to see the passengers off." Millie pointed to the trays of decadent breakfast treats. "Looks like you have some yummy good-bye goodies for the stragglers who are reluctant to say bon voyage."

"Gotta make sure they're eager to come back for more." Annette piled the last croissant on the tray and loaded it onto the cart before a kitchen worker wheeled it out of the galley. "What's on your agenda today?"

"After the gangway good-byes, I'm going to run down to maintenance to try to talk some sense into Sharky before he heads out for his date with Svetlana."

"I don't understand why you're so concerned about this date. He'll find out soon enough if she's legit. Want one?" Annette offered Millie a cream cheese Danish.

"No, thanks. I have a bad feeling about Svetlana, and I can't shake it. I'm also here to find out about your doctor's appointment and if you want me to go with you."

Annette motioned with her hands and lowered her voice. "It's at eleven. I already checked out the location. The office is within walking distance of the ship."

"You shouldn't go alone, especially after last night's incident." She told her friend about being scared by the homeless man and then later, Nikki's attack and robbery.

"I heard about Nikki but not what happened to you. Do you think it was the same person?"

"No." Millie tapped the tip of her chin. "My gut tells me it wasn't him. Why would he warn us about walking around after dark and then turn around and attack Nikki?"

"Drugs?" Annette shrugged.

"I suppose it's possible." Millie changed the subject. "So? Do you want me to go with you to your appointment? I don't think you should go alone."

Annette tilted her head as she considered Millie's offer. "Okay. Sure. You can go with me if you want to."

"Absolutely," Millie beamed. "I'll meet you down by the gangway at ten-thirty. It will give us plenty of time to get there." Her steps were lighter as she made her way out of the galley.

Annette had been tight-lipped about her reason for Doctor Gundervan's referral, and even if she never told Millie what was going on, Millie believed it was important for her friend to have someone with her.

She made it to the promenade gangway on deck five with several minutes to spare. Andy joined her a short time later. "You're early."

"I have a busy day planned," Millie glanced around. "Where's Sophia this morning?"

"She's working with Danielle. I was going to put her with you again, but..." Andy abruptly stopped.

"But what?" Millie prompted.

"She...uh. I thought it was best for her to spend time training with Danielle and some of the other entertainment staff." Andy's ears turned bright red, a sure sign he was fibbing.

"And what did she say about working with me?"

"Well." Andy cleared his throat. "She thinks you have the fluff jobs and told me she wasn't learning anything. She wants to do something with more substance."

Millie could feel her cheeks burn. "She said I have the fluff jobs?"

"She doesn't understand," Andy hurried on. "Sophia is new at this. It's going to take time for her to catch on and come to the realization there's no such thing as a fluff job on a cruise ship. We need to cut her some slack."

Millie muttered under her breath.

Andy started to comment but was interrupted by the first group of passengers, the diamond elites, who were being escorted to the exit. She pasted a smile on her face, greeting those she knew by name.

Although it was a large group, they knew the drill and moved fast to depart the ship. Up next were the diamond level passengers followed by the platinum level. They announced general passenger disembarkation, and there were only a few stragglers left.

"I think we hit some sort of record." Millie glanced at her app watch. "Less than two hours flat."

"And now we have some much-needed downtime. I heard about last night's incident and poor Nikki Tan's attack. Are you getting off the ship today?"

"I am. Annette and I have something to take care of. What are you doing?"

"Staff meetings, tweaking the new entertainment schedule."

A movement behind Andy caught Millie's eye. It was Sophia, and she was coming toward them. "Sophia is heading this way. I'll see you later." She didn't wait for a reply before pivoting on her heel and stalking off.

Her aggravation at Sophia's comments quickly faded. Perhaps Andy was right, and Millie needed to give her a chance. She forced the troublesome woman from her thoughts and headed to the nearest set of stairs. It was time to stop by Sharky's office to chat about his plans for meeting his Russian girlfriend.

Millie reached the entrance to the maintenance office, where the overpowering aroma of pine and new car smell filled the corridor. She gave the door a quick rap and stuck her head inside.

She almost burst out laughing at the sight of Sharky. "What on earth?"

"Hey, Millie." Sharky scooched around the side of his desk, the aroma becoming even more pungent.

"What is that smell?"

"It's the smell of a wealthy, successful man," Sharky smoothed his hair. "What do you think it smells like?"

"Like someone dumped a bottle of Lysol inside a new car." Millie clamped a hand over her mouth. "Good grief."

"Too much?"

Millie nodded as her eyes started to water.

"It'll wear off by the time I meet Svetlana." Sharky did a slow turn, swiveling his hips. "Well?"

"I like seersucker. I like plaid. The combination is…interesting."

"Does it scream wealthy, successful businessman?" Sharky asked hopefully.

"I…I'm not sure how Russian women gauge men's attire and smell," Millie answered honestly. "When and where are you meeting Svetlana?"

"We're meeting at a pub a coupla blocks from here. Cork & Olive at three." Sharky adjusted his bowtie. "You think the bowtie is too much?"

"No. The polka-dot bowtie goes nicely with the seersucker and plaid," Millie teased. "Seriously, if Svetlana judges a book by its cover, then she doesn't deserve you. Are you sure you want to do this?"

"Of course."

She could tell from the look on Sharky's face he was determined to meet Svetlana and knew no amount of persuading was going to stop him. "I hope you know what you're getting yourself into."

"I got this, Millie. Svetlana is gonna be the best thing that ever happened to Sherman Kiveski."

"Then I hope she's everything you dreamed of." Millie backed out of the office, offering a silent prayer he knew what he was doing. Still, she couldn't see the harm if she happened to "swing by" the pub to check on him.

Chapter 6

The early morning passed quickly, beginning with a meeting for all entertainment staff in the theater. Andy laid out his plans for the new passengers' activities for the summer months.

He introduced a group of Celtic dancers who would be replacing Blackjack Blaze's SeaFi show. Millie briefly wondered how Blaze's IRS case ended and had almost forgotten the man was in some sort of trouble back in the States.

Andy droned on about the revised schedule. He reminded them of Isla's promotion and then motioned for Sophia to join him on stage.

Millie could've sworn the woman batted her eyes at Andy before stepping close to him, so close they were almost touching.

He gave Sophia a lopsided grin before turning his attention to his staff members. "Siren of the Seas is fortunate to have Ms. Williams on board for the summer while we're visiting the Isles. Sophia is a former history teacher. She'll be offering port talks for each of our stops. Please stop by to introduce yourself. I'll let her say a few words."

Sophia returned Andy's smile as she took the microphone. "I'm thrilled to be on board Siren of the Seas cruise ship for the season. I was born and raised in London, but have traveled extensively to Ireland, Scotland and the beautiful Isles." She ended by stating she hoped to get to know the staff and crew on board and handed the mic back to Andy.

Danielle, who was standing next to Millie, leaned in. "She's so full of herself. We stopped by the coffee bar this morning, and she actually had the nerve to tell Carlah she was making the iced lattes wrong."

"I thought tea was more of the favored British drink," Millie whispered back.

"This lady thinks she's an expert on everything."

"She told Andy I get all of the 'fluff' jobs."

"Really?" Danielle lifted a brow. "She's a trip."

Millie grew quiet as Andy wrapped up the meeting with a mention of Nikki Tan's attack and a word of caution about being out after dark and wandering around alone.

Danielle and Millie stood off to the side to wait for the room to clear.

"I guess it's time to retrieve my protégé."

"Better you than me." Millie gave her friend's arm a reassuring squeeze before Danielle reluctantly trudged down the aisle to join Andy and Sophia.

Millie wandered out of the theater, her thoughts turning to Annette's upcoming doctor's appointment. Not only was Annette's appointment weighing heavy on her mind, but Sharky's date and Nikki's attack were as well.

The outer corridor was empty and quiet, almost too quiet. She already missed the hustle and bustle of activities, greeting and interacting with the passengers, making sure they were enjoying their vacations.

She also missed the familiar routine of the embarkation day. Although hectic, it was one of her favorites. The new passengers arrived, many overwhelmed by the tedious boarding process. It all started at the port - a madhouse on turnover days with thousands of passengers struggling to gather their belongings and track down their transportation while thousands more were starting to arrive.

Majestic Cruise Lines enlisted a small army of port security, who worked alongside the port employees, moving people to and from the ship. It was non-stop motion and noise with local police hired to keep traffic and pedestrians moving, not to mention taxis, shuttle buses and those who arrived on their own.

Making it to the port was only the beginning. Next up was tracking down a porter to load luggage on the massive carts headed for the ship's cargo hold.

With enormous effort behind the scenes, the cruise line worked hard to assist the guests, some of whom knew the drill while others were traveling on Siren of the Seas for the first time.

After leaving their luggage with designated porters, passengers either found their own way or were directed to security checkpoints. The seasoned cruisers with VIP status were given their own special boarding area where the atmosphere was less chaotic.

General boarding was the complete opposite, and at times a scene of total chaos. Similar to airport terminals, passengers were required to pass through security screening areas, sometimes being asked to remove clothing and shoes, scanning their carry-ons, checking passports and boarding passes.

After the first hurdle of security, passengers joined the long lines that snaked back and forth where cruise ship employees checked them in, confirmed their onboard charge accounts and printed their sail and sign cards. Although most had pre-assigned cabins, there was always a small group of passengers who chose guaranteed cabins, which were assigned only hours before the ship's departure.

With a picture taken, passengers were almost home free, passing by the first of many of the ship's photographers and a gigantic cutout of the cruise ship. They were handed a life preserver emblazoned with the ship's name, forcing either a weary smile or a triumphant smile of victory at having finally arrived.

The last step was boarding the ship - what Millie considered the highlight of the first day. Up the gangway they traveled, zigzagging back and forth, going higher and higher until they reached the ship's entrance where Andy and Millie waited to welcome them.

After the first day, passengers began settling into the ship's routine, and the stressed-out looks were replaced with relaxed smiles. The pace was slower, not as hectic. The guests had finally arrived at "ship time."

But the frantic boarding process was still a couple of days away. She wandered into Sky Chapel where she found two crewmembers painting baseboard trim. She gave them a small smile and started to back out of the sanctuary when she spotted Pastor Pete Evans standing near the podium.

He waved Millie to the front. "I figured you would be off the ship, shopping up a storm," he teased.

"I'm leaving soon but still had a few minutes, so I thought I would stop by here for some quiet time. The chapel is getting a minor facelift." Millie motioned to the workers.

"It needed a little sprucing up. Since we don't have passengers, some of the delayed maintenance is being done now." The pastor smiled apologetically. "My office is free if you'd like to chat for a minute."

"Sure. I'm meeting Annette near the gangway at ten-thirty." Millie followed the pastor to his small office in the back.

The two of them chatted about the crossing and then Pastor Pete's plans for the next couple of days. He told Millie he'd promised to purchase some souvenirs for his grandchildren. His granddaughter had specifically requested an authentic British tea set.

The conversation drifted to Nikki's attack the previous evening. "Hopefully, it was an isolated incident." Millie mentioned the confrontation with the homeless man and his warning to the women. "We're not off to a good start."

"No, we're not. We'll all need to be careful when exploring the port area." The pastor gazed over

Millie's head. "The maintenance crew has finished if you'd like a few moments alone."

"Yes, I think I would." Millie slowly stood. "Thanks for the chat. I always feel better after spending time here." She thanked him again and made her way back to the chapel. It was dark except for a single strand of twinkling lights that ran along the back of the platform.

She sank onto an empty bench and clasped her hands, staring at the cross. Millie lowered her head and closed her eyes. She prayed for Annette's doctor's appointment and Sharky's date with Svetlana. She prayed for Nikki's healing and the homeless man. She also prayed for Sophia, that she and the woman would get along. Her last prayer was for her family, now thousands of miles away.

Millie forced her thoughts of the distance from her mind and ended the prayer by thanking God for her many blessings...a loving husband and family, good health, wonderful friends and a dream job.

As she stood, she was filled with a sense of peace. Annette would be all right. Sharky would survive his date with Svetlana. She had no idea how she could help the poor homeless man, but Millie decided she needed to give it some thought. The stranger may very well have saved them from an attack.

Annette was already waiting...or more like pacing...back and forth along the dock when Millie arrived. Her expression was strained and her face pale.

"You okay?" Millie asked worriedly.

"Yeah. I'm fine." Annette began walking, and Millie fell into step. "I have an aversion to doctors, hospitals, needles, the whole kit and caboodle."

"It'll be okay." Millie's assurance rang hollow, not knowing the purpose of the doctor's visit. From what little she'd gleaned from Annette, Doctor Gundervan was insistent she keep the appointment he'd made for her when they reached the UK.

"How far away is the doctor's office?" Millie asked.

"It's a clinic. Two more blocks." Annette's face turned a splotchy red, and she started wheezing.

"We can slow down. We're making good time."

"Right." Annette slowed. "I'm just ready to get this over with."

"I'm sure you are. I prayed about it a few minutes ago. God has this."

Annette stopped in front of a drab, gray building. Etched on the double doors were several doctors' names. She pulled a small slip of paper from her jacket pocket and unfolded it. "Dr. William Corbette."

"I see his name. It's right there." Millie pointed to one of the names emblazoned on the front of the door. She lifted her gaze, her heart plummeting when she realized what kind of clinic it was.

Chapter 7

"Southampton Cardiology Clinic. You're here to see a heart doctor."

"Yep." Annette approached the receptionist desk and jotted her name on the sign-in sheet while Millie wandered over to the waiting area and found a seat near the back.

Annette joined her moments later and began filling out the paperwork the woman had given her. She was halfway back to the front desk when the side door slowly opened. "Annette Delacroix."

Millie gave her friend an encouraging smile and a thumbs up. It wasn't until she disappeared behind the door that the smile vanished, replaced by an anxious expression.

A cardiologist...it all made sense. Annette had been complaining she'd been having bouts of fatigue and dizziness, not to mention shortness of breath. Millie had chalked it up to her friend's stressful job as the ship's director of food and beverage. She was on the go 24/7, rarely taking time off unless forced to.

Millie slid out of the chair and slowly walked to the window, staring blankly at the street. Annette had always been tough as nails, no-nonsense...a true friend. She selfishly wondered what she would do if Annette was forced to retire and give up her beloved job on board Siren of the Seas.

She'd come to depend on her friend on so many levels. Millie couldn't imagine life on board the ship without her. She slipped back into the chair and reached for a magazine, mindlessly flipping through the pages before tossing it on the side table.

Patients came and went. In fact, several came in after them and were long gone while Millie still waited.

Two and a half long hours dragged by, and Millie was in mini panic mode. What if the doctor had examined Annette, determined she was in a dire situation and planned to admit her to the nearest hospital?

The terrifying thought made her feel lightheaded. Needing some air, Millie darted outside and onto the sidewalk where she began to pace. She waited for the spell to subside before returning to the waiting room.

Millie made a beeline for the reception desk. "Yes. My friend has been at her appointment for over two hours now. I was wondering if there was a way to check on her."

The woman at the desk smiled. "What is your friend's name?"

"Annette Delacroix."

"I'll see what I can find out." The woman slipped out of the reception area and returned a short time later. "Your friend will be out shortly."

"Thank you." Millie returned to her seat and waited another half an hour, glancing at her watch every couple of minutes. Finally, a pale Annette emerged. She approached the reception desk to have a brief word with the woman, who handed her a card.

Millie popped out of the chair and waited for her near the exit. "I was worried sick. I finally sent the receptionist back to check on you."

"I'm sorry it took so long. They ran the gamut...a stress test, chest x-ray, blood work. I have to come back next time we're in port for the results." Annette stepped onto the sidewalk, and Millie joined her.

"What does the doctor think it is?"

"Best case is angina. Gundervan mentioned angina, too. I've been doing some research on natural herbal remedies."

"Is it wise to try herbal stuff before an actual diagnosis?" Millie wrinkled her nose.

"I don't see how it could hurt. Hawthorn berries are a popular herb for heart conditions. I found out about it when I was doing some online research. They call it a supportive treatment for heart-related conditions."

"How are you going to get your hands on hawthorn berries? It's not like there's an herbal store in the middle of the ocean."

"I don't need a store." Annette slowed her pace as they reached the end of the block. "The berries grow wild on the Emerald Isle."

"Ireland," Millie guessed.

"Yep...and guess who's heading to the Emerald Isle this week?" Annette didn't wait for a reply. "We are, but I don't have time off. Amit offered to get off the ship in Cork to search for the berries. The only problem is that I don't want him going alone."

"I'm visiting Blarney Castle. Hey." Millie abruptly stopped, excitedly popping her friend in the arm. "What about the Poison Garden at Blarney?"

Annette chuckled. "You're going to pick a bunch of poisonous plants to take me out?"

"No. I read somewhere that they also have herbal gardens. Amit can go to Blarney with me. While we're off the ship, we'll see if we can track down some hawthorn berries. Even if we can't find them at Blarney, I'm sure we'll find them somewhere."

"Are...you sure? I don't want you to spend what little time you have off hunting down a bunch of berries for me."

"Annette Delacroix," Millie chided, "if you think hawthorn berries might help you, I'll do whatever I can to find them."

The women reached a street filled with restaurants and small shops. It was the same one Cat, Danielle and Millie had visited the previous evening.

"That would be awesome. I...I don't know how to thank you. I owe you one."

"I've already figured out a way for you to pay me back," Millie motioned toward the touristy area. "But first, let's grab a bite to eat. My treat."

87

The women settled on a quaint and cozy tea shop. Once inside, they ordered crumpets to go along with their mint tea. The food was delivered on a small plate, along with a piping hot pot of tea.

"This is it?" Millie reached for a crumpet that looked somewhat similar to an English muffin.

"What we call crumpets are your American version of the English muffin," the server explained in a clipped British accent. "Although crumpets are cooked on a hot griddle." She pointed out the various toppings...butter, bacon, cheese, jam and clotted cream. "Butter is one of the more popular crumpet toppings."

Annette thanked the woman and waited for her to leave. She sipped the tea and reached for the small knife, slathering a thick layer of clotted cream on top before taking a bite. "Tasty. You should try it."

Millie carefully placed a crumpet in the center of her small plate and spread a thin layer of butter over the top. The crumpet's center was spongy, and it had a yeasty flavor. "Not bad, although there's not much difference between this and a muffin."

"Agreed."

The women polished off the small plate of food, with Millie sampling the jam before declaring she was full. She waited for Annette to finish the last one. "What time do you start your shift?"

"At four. I gave as many of my staff time off as possible and warned them to be careful while in port." Annette downed the rest of her tea. "I suppose we should head back to the ship unless you want to go shopping, although you know wandering around stores looking for stuff that I don't need isn't my thing."

"No." Millie picked up the bill. "I do have something else in mind. You know how you said you owe me one?"

"Yeah," Annette nodded suspiciously. "Let me guess. You already thought of something."

"Since you don't have to work until four, I figured you could go with me while I check on Sharky."

"Sharky?"

Millie hurried on. "I'm concerned about his date with Svetlana. He's meeting her at a place called the Cork & Olive at three. It's not far from here. I want to swing by there to make sure he's not getting in over his head."

"He's an adult. You've already warned him. If he's determined to hook up with this woman, I say let him."

"But I don't think she's legit," Millie insisted. "He's been sending her money. I hate to say it, but he showed me a picture of her, and she's not his type."

Annette chuckled. "What is Sharky's type?"

"Please go with me. Just this once."

Annette rolled her eyes. "Fine, but we're only staying long enough to confirm he's all right. I don't want to hang around for the whole date. Besides, like I said, I have to be back on board by four."

"Perfect," Millie beamed. "Thanks, Annette. You're the best."

"I'm doing this for you, not Sharky."

"Right." Millie popped out of her chair and darted to the checkout counter. She paid the bill and joined Annette, who was waiting for her near the door. "We have to figure out where the Cork & Olive is located."

They stepped onto the sidewalk, and Millie pulled her cell phone from her purse. She typed in the bar's name and pressed enter. With a quick click for the directions, the women were on their way. "We're even closer than I thought. All we have to do is take a shortcut through the park, make a right and the bar is on the corner."

They arrived in front of the bar at two-fifty. Millie hovered off to the side.

"I feel like a stalker," Annette joked.

"Me too."

Annette eased in next to her. "You see them?"

"I see Sharky. He's at a table in the corner. He's alone," Millie reported.

"Maybe she'll be a no-show."

"On the one hand, I hope so. On the other hand, for Sharky's sake, I hope she's everything he's dreamed of."

Annette peered around the corner and in the window. "Good grief. What on earth is that man wearing?"

"Seersucker pants, a plaid shirt, a polka-dotted bowtie and a cologne that would give most people a migraine."

"Oh, brother. Well, if she was on the fence about him online, wait until she meets him in person."

"He said he wanted to make sure he stood out from the crowd."

"Stood out? When I close my eyes, I can still see him."

"Hang on." Millie motioned with her hand. "Someone walked over to the table. No way."

Chapter 8

"What is it?" Annette nudged Millie. "Well, will you look at that? If that's Svetlana, we're gonna nickname her Svetlana the Giant."

"No kidding." Millie watched as Sharky scrambled out of his chair, a bouquet of flowers in his hand. He handed them to the woman. "It has to be her. Unless he handed someone else flowers."

Sharky gallantly offered the woman his seat and then slid in next to her. From where she stood, Millie could see she was a blond. The color of her hair was similar to the woman in the online picture Sharky had shown her.

"Is this the woman he showed you?" Annette asked.

"I can't be certain. She had blond hair. I remember that much." Millie squinted her eyes, feeling slightly guilty for spying on them.

"I say we give them five minutes, tops, and then we can leave in good conscience, knowing you made sure Sharky was safe."

"Or maybe ten. I'm not getting a warm and fuzzy feeling." Millie grew quiet as she continued to watch. She couldn't get a reading on Sharky's feelings. His expression was measured. "He doesn't strike me as overly-ecstatic."

Annette shifted her feet and consulted her watch. "This spy mission is a success. I say we head back to the ship."

"Give me another minute or two." Millie motioned for Annette to wait. "Sharky's going somewhere. He left the table. It looks like he's headed to the restrooms."

Svetlana turned as she watched Sharky leave, giving Millie a clear view of her side profile. Her eyes were drawn to the woman's thick, bushy eyebrows. Her hair was parted down the middle and twisted into two buns, one on each side of her head. "I can see part of her face."

"Let me have a look." Annette stepped back in front of the window.

"I thought you didn't care."

"I don't. Whoa. Look at her hairdo! It looks like she has two small spaceships growing out of the sides of her head."

"Kind of," Millie agreed.

"Hang on. She's doing something. She's switching drinks with him."

"You're kidding."

"Nope. That's interesting."

"What should we do?"

"Irritate him by making an appearance and warning him about the drink switcheroo." Annette slung her backpack over her shoulder and began walking inside.

Millie was right behind her.

An employee met them near the door. "Party of two?"

"No. We're meeting friends." Annette sidestepped the woman. They walked past the bar, making their way to the back where they approached the table. "Hello."

The woman turned. Her eyes shifted from Annette to Millie, a puzzled expression on her face.

Millie didn't wait for an invitation and eased into a chair across from Svetlana. Now that she was face-to-face with the woman, she realized she was much younger than the picture she'd seen. "You're here with Sharky."

"You know him?" The woman lifted a unibrow.

"We work with him on board Siren of the Seas."
Annette pointed to Sharky's drink. "We watched
you switch drinks as we were coming in."

An unreadable expression crossed the
woman's...person's face. Svetlana's chiseled chin
and square forehead struck Millie as more
masculine than feminine. Her voice was deep and
more of a breathy whisper as if she were trying to
talk softly.

"I don't know vut you are talking abowt."

"What's going on?" Sharky returned to the table,
a scowl on his face. "What are you two doing here?"

"We're here to warn you," Annette said bluntly.
"We watched this woman switch drinks with you a
moment ago."

"Maybe mine tastes better," he said.

"Dis is crazy." Svetlana snatched her purse off the
table and shoved her chair back. It teetered before
hitting the floor with a loud bang. "I thought

meeting you might be a mistake. You have some crazy employees." She stomped out of the bar.

"Wait!" Sharky ran after her.

Millie watched as the couple stopped in front of the large picture window. Sharky gestured wildly, a look of pleading on his face while Svetlana shook her head. After a few tense moments, the woman walked away.

Sharky returned inside, a thunderous expression on his face.

"I think we're in trouble," Millie said. "Sharky doesn't look happy."

"What was that all about?"

"We were trying to save you. We watched you leave the table. While you were gone, your beloved swapped drinks. We thought you should know what she did."

"You're making a mountain out of a molehill." Sharky jabbed his finger at Annette. "And you're full of sour grapes because our relationship hit the skids, and now you're trying to ruin any chance I have with Svetlana."

He snatched the drink off the table and carried it to the bar. He pointed toward the women and handed it to the bartender, who promptly dumped it in the sink, before marching back. "You two busybodies need to find someone else to stalk."

"We're not stalking you. We're concerned friends." Millie paused. "Did you take a good, hard look at Svetlana? She's not the woman you met on the internet. This was a different person."

"So she put on a little weight," Sharky argued. "The picture is a few years old. We all change."

"I...she's not who you think she is..." Millie's voice trailed off. She could tell from the look on his face he wasn't listening to a word she was saying. "We were only trying to protect you."

Sharky turned his accusing stare on Annette. "This is your fault. You couldn't get me back, so you decided no one else can have me."

"Oh, brother." Annette briefly closed her eyes. "I'm only here as a favor to Millie, who was concerned for your safety and, I might add, it appears for very good reason."

"I'm perfectly safe. I plan to call Svetlana later to smooth things over." Sharky began making his way toward the exit and the women trailed behind.

He waited for them on the sidewalk. "I'm only gonna say this once. Butt out and mind your own business." He stormed off.

The women waited until he rounded the corner and disappeared from sight.

"That went over well," Annette said.

"Like a lead balloon," Millie said miserably. "We were only trying to save him from a bad situation."

"And ended up making matters worse. I get a bad vibe off that lady...and I use the term lady loosely. She has some masculine attributes."

"Was it the chiseled features or the deep, breathy voice?"

"Both, among other things."

Millie fell into step, and they began making their way back to the ship. "Why do you think she switched drinks?"

Annette shrugged. "Who knows? Maybe she put something in his drink and we missed that part. Could be she planned to drug Sharky and then rob him. You said he's already given her money."

"According to Reef, he was sending her money so she could travel here. Who knows how much he's given her? But why travel to another country just to rob a cruise ship employee? She can rob people in her own backyard and skip the plane ride." A sudden thought occurred to Millie. "What if...what if her plan is to somehow sneak on board the Siren of the Seas and return to the States with us?"

"As a stowaway?" Annette shook her head. "Security is too tight. Maybe she thinks Sharky will put in a good word for her and the cruise line will hire her."

The women discussed the possibility, thinking that maybe the woman's goal was to reach the United States. The major hurdle would be making it through the cruise line's rigorous hiring process. It wasn't impossible. In fact, the majority of the ship's crewmembers were non-American.

"It still doesn't explain why she switched drinks," Annette pointed out.

The women reached the ship, dinging their keycards as they boarded the gangway. Annette thanked her friend for accompanying her to the doctor's appointment.

"I have plenty of time before my evening tasks. I think I'll swing by and chat with Amit about the trip to Blarney Castle. Before I do that, I want to drop my things off at home."

Millie made a quick stop by the apartment to let Scout out before heading downstairs to the galley. When she arrived, she found Amit and Annette bustling back and forth.

Much to her surprise, Brody, one of the nightshift security guards, was also there. He was sitting on a stool, hunched over a side counter, eating cake...and not just a single slice. He was chowing down on an entire sheet cake.

Millie gave Annette a wave and made her way over to Brody. "Hey, Brody."

"Hey, Millie." Brody scooped up a large forkful of cake and shoveled it into his mouth. "What's up?"

"I'm here to see Amit." Millie leaned an elbow on the counter and watched him devour another large chunk of chocolate cake. "How're you doing?"

"I'm okay." Brody shrugged. "Patterson's got us working double shifts since Nikki's attack."

"I'm sure he does. So how's everything else?"

"Everything is dandy." Brody polished off the last bite. "I better get going."

Annette hurried over. "You're leaving already, Brody?"

"Yeah. I got a meeting in a few. Thanks for the cake and everything else."

"You're welcome." Annette patted his arm. "The swinging doors are always open if you want to chat."

"I appreciate it, Annette." Brody let out a small belch. "Excuse me." He gave Millie a small nod and ambled out of the galley.

Millie placed a hand on her hip and watched him leave. "What was that all about?"

"Brody is drowning his sorrows in chocolate," Annette joked.

"Sorrows?"

"He's still pining over Danielle and their breakup. He stops by here at least once a week for a shoulder to cry on."

"I had no idea. I always wondered what happened. Danielle and Brody seemed perfect for each other."

"I..." Annette started to say something and quickly clammed up.

"You know what happened."

"Maybe. Yes. But I'm sworn to secrecy."

"Brody didn't want to break up with Danielle."

"Nope, and reading between the lines, neither did she. It was a misunderstanding. I wish I could figure out a way to get them alone together. I've tried. Unfortunately, they're both stubborn as mules."

Millie placed her hands on her cheeks, thoughtfully eyeing the galley door. "You think if we could figure out a way to get the two of them together in the same room to talk, they might be able to patch things up?"

"It's possible. I've been thinking about it for a while now. Not that I mind Brody devouring a dessert in one sitting, but I think he and Danielle need to have a little heart to heart."

"I see." Millie absentmindedly picked up the dirty fork Brody had left behind. "You know what? I think I have an idea...an absolutely brilliant idea."

Chapter 9

"You're gonna play matchmaker," Annette guessed.

"No. *We're* gonna play matchmaker," Millie corrected. "I have a little planning to do. Give me an hour or so. It will involve a romantic dinner, some candlelight and an empty galley with a corner table for two."

Annette chuckled. "You are a mastermind. I like it. I like it a lot."

Amit made his way over, a harried expression on his face. "Miss Annette. I need you to taste the shepherd's pie. Something is not right."

"Did you add curry again?" Annette pursed her lips.

"Only a little bit." Amit pinched his thumb and index finger together. "It taste too bland. It need some...how do you say? Zip."

"You cannot put curry in shepherd's pie."

"Amit." Millie patted his arm. "We need to talk about the port stop in Cork / Cobh. I'm going to go with you to pick up Annette's hawthorn berries, but we can discuss it later."

She told her friends good-bye, and Annette barely gave her a glance as she continued to lecture Amit on why he couldn't add curry to the dish.

Amit gave Millie a quick wink, all the while nodding his head as Annette continued talking.

Millie's next stop was the guest services desk to see if Nikki was around and to check on her friend. The desk was empty, which didn't surprise her since there were no passengers on board who needed help.

Instead, Millie decided to drop by Donovan Sweeney's office, which was located directly behind guest services. She rapped lightly, eased the door open and stuck her head around the corner.

"Millie." Donovan waved her in. "Come in." He waited for her to have a seat. "Are you enjoying your day off?"

"I am. I ran an errand with Annette, and then we checked in on Sharky and his date."

"That's right. I forgot about Sharky's new girlfriend." Donovan leaned back in his chair, the smile on his face widening. "How did his Russian date go?"

"It was...over fast." Millie blurted out what had happened. "He's not very happy with Annette and me. He defended the woman the entire time, insisting we were trying to ruin his date."

"For what purpose?"

"Because he's convinced himself Annette is after him."

"That's crazy."

"Yep. Anyhoo, it blew up in our faces. He plans on meeting Svetlana again, and who knows what will happen."

Donovan's phone rang, and he held up a finger. "Donovan Sweeney speaking. Yes. I'll be on the bridge shortly." He hung up the phone. "Staff meeting on the bridge. Was there anything else?"

"I thought I would check on Nikki after last night's attack."

"She's fine, although rightfully shaken. I doubt she'll get off the ship again anytime soon."

"I'm sorry to hear that. Not a good way to start off at a new port. I'll walk with you. I'm heading to the bridge myself."

While they walked, they discussed the exciting new itinerary and then Sophia's arrival, to which Millie decided to keep her thoughts to herself.

They reached the bridge where several officers were already gathered around the conference table.

Millie greeted them with a wave but never slowed until she reached the apartment.

Once inside, Millie switched the computer on. She checked her emails and their bank accounts before surfing the internet for local news, wondering if perhaps there was a mention about the recent attack. There was nothing, and she figured that perhaps the local officials decided to keep it out of the news so they wouldn't scare off the tourists.

Cruising was a big business in Southampton. Not only was Siren of the Seas departing from the port, but several other major cruise lines called it home for the summer months, as well.

She finished up, and Scout began circling her legs, letting out a small whine. "Would you like to visit the park across the street?"

Scout pawed at Millie's shoe. "I guess that's a 'yes.'" Since there was still plenty of daylight hours left and the area was bustling with other pedestrians and visitors, Millie decided it was safe to venture out.

They exited the ship, stopping twice for crewmembers who greeted Scout. She carried him across the street and through the gate. When they reached the park, Millie set him in a grassy area a safe distance away from the busy sidewalk.

He pranced around, unaccustomed to the feel of grass on his paws. It didn't take long for him to start exploring the nearby trees before trotting over to a flower garden. He kicked up small tufts of dirt, a look of pure joy on his face.

"You love the grass and trees and dirt," Millie chuckled. "Maybe we should see if maintenance can install a small garden for you, right next to your miniature pool oasis."

Scout began tugging on his leash. Millie let him lead her through the park as he scoped out the scenery. Although the park was surrounded by bustling city streets, it was easy to block out the noise and focus on the park's serene setting, picturesque flower gardens and towering shade trees filled with chirping birds.

It felt good to be on solid ground with trees, grass and flowers, something others took for granted but something Millie appreciated since she spent most of her days on board the ship. She loved ship life, but a change of pace was refreshing.

Millie let Scout wander until he tired, and then they crossed back over to the port. The security checkpoint was in sight, and Millie slowed. *Beep.* A loud beeping sound caught her attention. Off to her right were bright flashing lights and police vehicles.

They changed course and began heading toward the cars parked in front of the abandoned warehouse where the homeless man had stopped them.

She crept closer, careful to keep a safe distance. Several officers surrounded a blanket that was lying on the ground. Underneath the blanket was a bulky object, the outline of a person if Millie were to guess.

Beyond the blanket, several people were moving back and forth inside the building. Millie's eyes scanned the crowd until she spied Dave Patterson talking to the port security and what appeared to be two local law enforcement officials.

Johar, one of the ship's security guards, walked by. Millie reached out to stop him. "What's going on?"

"One of our security guards was patrolling the area a short time ago. He thought he heard a noise coming from inside the warehouse. He decided to investigate and found an injured homeless man."

"Oh, no." Millie started to ask about the man's condition when an ambulance came screeching around the corner.

The crowd parted to make room for the emergency personnel, who sprang from the vehicle and jogged over to the blanket. They knelt on either side. From where she stood, Millie could see sparse patches of gray hair. One of the men opened his emergency kit and removed several items.

She shifted Scout to her other arm when her scheduler app alerted her it was time for her to head back to the ship for the first of several staff meetings. Millie offered a silent prayer that the injured man would be okay before reluctantly making her way to the security checkpoint.

The guard patted Scout's head as he greeted Millie. "It's nice to see Scout enjoying the beautiful day."

"We visited the park across the street. Scout loved every minute of it." Millie nodded toward the warehouse. "The homeless man who hangs around the warehouse was injured."

"He was." The guard's expression grew solemn. "First, Nikki's attack and now this. I'm beginning to wonder how safe this area is."

"You're not alone." Millie finished passing through and hurried back on board, where she made a beeline for the atrium. She rounded the corner and nearly collided head-on with Sophia, who was coming from the opposite direction.

"There you are." The woman patted Scout's head. "What a cute little dog. I didn't know animals were allowed on board the ship."

"They're not. The captain made an exception. Were you looking for me?"

"I was. Andy mentioned you had vouchers for the ship's spa. I was hoping to try several of their services before the passengers arrive."

"Of course." Millie glanced at her watch. "I...I'll try to grab a few when I'm upstairs. I'm running behind for Andy's meeting."

"I see." Sophia's expression soured. "I'm sorry to bother you."

"No bother. Andy's a stickler about being prompt." She cast the woman an apologetic smile and hurried to the apartment to drop Scout off and switch back into her work uniform.

She darted across the bridge and then remembered the spa vouchers Sophia had asked about. She returned home, rummaging around in the desk drawer until she found a handful.

Millie ran down the stairs, not slowing until she reached the main theater floor. Andy's office light was on, and the door open when Millie arrived. Danielle, Isla and Sophia were already inside.

"Glad you could join us, Millie," Andy teased.

"I'm right on time. These are for you." Millie placed the slips of paper on the table next to Sophia.

"Where were you?"

"I took Scout to the park across the street." She briefly filled them in on the return trip to the ship and the unfolding scene at the abandoned warehouse. "I think it may have been the man who stopped Cat, Danielle and me last night."

Danielle's eyes grew wide. "Is he all right?"

"I don't know. The paramedics or whatever they call them here were working on him when I left."

There was a brief discussion...mainly a lecture from Andy on not wandering off in areas at night and alone, followed by a reminder about Nikki's attack. "From now on, I don't think any of you should leave the ship unless you're with someone, and it's during the daylight hours."

"The buddy system," Isla said. "Stick together is safe together."

"Yes." Andy steered the conversation to his plans for the first group of passengers, who were scheduled to arrive on Friday. Much to Millie's relief, he'd decided to have Sophia spend time with Isla to go over some of the highlights of the upcoming port stops.

"I think that's a wonderful idea," Millie gushed. "It makes more sense for Isla and Sophia to work together."

Isla shot Millie a perturbed look and attempted to kick her under the table.

Millie, anticipating the move, shifted her legs, making sure she was out of reach.

"Is there a problem?" Andy lifted his head.

"No. Not at all." Millie smiled innocently. "Sorry to interrupt."

The meeting ended with Andy assigning each of them a different area of the ship. They were to inspect and inventory the entertainment materials and supplies, to make sure everything was in working order.

Isla and Sophia left first. Danielle was next. Millie began following them out when Andy stopped her. "I would like a word with you, Millie." He motioned for her to close the door and waited until she resumed her spot at the table. "Is anything troubling you?"

"You mean more than usual?" Millie joked. She quickly sobered at the look on her boss's face. "No. Everything is hunky-dory. I'm out of my funk and looking forward to the summer. Why? Do I seem troubled?"

"Sophia mentioned you were a little...irritated when she stopped you a short time ago to ask a question. I thought if there was something going on, we could nip it in the bud and get you back on track."

"Irritated?" Millie's eyebrows furrowed. "Scout and I were on our way back to the apartment after witnessing a disturbing scene near the docking area when Sophia stopped me. I was running behind and in a hurry since you're a stickler for being on time. I may have been distracted, but I most certainly wasn't irritated."

"Sophia is trying hard to fit in and perhaps she's a little sensitive to her surroundings. It may take her a few days to become accustomed to the quirkiness of Americans."

"What's that supposed to mean...quirkiness of Americans?"

"She said you were loud, almost yelling."

"Yelling?"

Andy pressed his palms together. "Americans tend to be a little louder than the English."

"Huh." Millie mulled over the comment, struggling to remember the precise tone she'd used with Sophia.

"You would be doing me a huge favor if you tried a little harder with her." Andy picked up his stack of papers and tapped them on the desk, his signal their meeting was over.

Millie eased out of her chair. "I'll try my best to remember to use my inside voice when she's around and be a little more understanding." *And avoid her like the plague*, she added silently.

"Thanks, Millie."

"Before I go, I was wondering if you could give me a couple of those fancy embossed fill-in-the-blank dinner invitations."

"These?" Andy reached into the cabinet behind him and removed a small stack of invitations.

"Those are the ones. I only need two." Millie took them from Andy.

"You're inviting someone to the apartment for dinner?"

"No. This is for something else." She thanked him for the invitations before exiting his office, pausing to study the list he'd given her, including the list of supplies and entertainment areas for her to inspect.

Millie tucked the list in her front pocket and ran a light hand over the invitations. She needed to get to work, but first, she would have to move fast to put her perfect plan into place.

Chapter 10

Millie's first call was to Annette. She briefly filled her friend in on the details of her matchmaking plan.

"This will be perfect," Annette gushed. "Brody doesn't start his shift until midnight. What about Danielle?"

Millie juggled her phone in one hand while she consulted the scheduling app. "Her schedule is almost identical to mine. She's working on inventorying. I'm sure she has downtime and some flexibility tonight."

"We need someone to deliver the invitations." Annette began to holler. "Hey, Amit! You wanna play matchmaker?"

Millie couldn't hear his reply. Annette returned. "Bring the invitations here, and I'll have Amit deliver them as soon as possible."

By the time Millie reached the galley, Annette had already enlisted the assistance of one of the kitchen staff who practiced calligraphy. It didn't take long for the woman to create two personalized invitations...one for Danielle and the other for Brody, each inviting the other to an impromptu dinner in the galley kitchen.

As soon as the ink dried, Annette handed the invitations to Amit and propelled him toward the galley door. "Find Brody first. He's probably hanging around somewhere near the security office or employee area. If you can't find him, have someone in Patterson's office track him down."

"Yes," Amit nodded.

Annette turned to Millie. "Where's Danielle right now?"

Millie consulted her scheduler. "She should be going over the dance classes at the Tahitian Nights Dance Club on deck eight."

"You heard her. Find Brody first, Danielle second. Don't come back until you have their verbal RSVP. Ten o'clock tonight."

"RSVP. Dinner at ten o'clock tonight," Amit repeated. "Got it."

"And remember, you're not to let them know who gave you these invitations."

"Yes, Miss Annette. My lips are zipped."

Millie chuckled. "We owe you one."

"I will be happy to do this. Brody, he is unhappy. He cannot afford to keep eating cake all of the time."

Millie watched Amit hurry out of the galley. "Do you think this will work?"

"Like gangbusters. They're both going to think the other invited them to dinner. We'll have plenty of time to get this place cleared out. My idea is a candlelit table for two, some romantic music to set the mood and a scrumptious meal."

"What are we serving?" Millie asked.

Annette drummed her fingers on the counter. "I've been giving it some thought. Cheesy baked shrimp scampi, French-cut green beans with almonds and twice-baked potatoes."

"What about dessert? You can't pull off a romantic dinner without dessert."

"Since Brody already polished off an entire double fudge chocolate cake, I decided to go with something a little lighter. It's one of my latest creations."

She led Millie to the prep counter. "They're caramel apple mini cheesecakes, guaranteed to make even the least romantic of men go ga-ga."

"It's not ready." Millie stared at the muffin tins. Inside was a creamy yellow mixture covering what appeared to be a graham cracker crust.

"Patience grasshopper." Annette grabbed a pair of gloves and slipped them on before reaching for a stainless steel mixing bowl. "I'm getting ready to put this batch in the oven. First, we add the final toppings."

"Which are?"

"A thinly-sliced Granny smith apple, although you can use ambrosia, golden delicious or a sweet honey crisp, too. Brown sugar, flour, oats, cinnamon, salt and butter."

"The same ingredients you would use for an apple crisp," Millie interrupted.

"Yes, but with one extra ingredient...chopped walnuts. So, we place the sliced apples in a single layer on top of the cheesecake and then add a thin layer of topping." Annette emptied the contents of the topping bowl and removed her gloves. "Next, we put the tins in the oven for about half an hour." She eased the muffin tins into the oven and shut the door.

Millie wrinkled her nose. "This seems like a lot of work."

"It is, which is why we won't be serving these in the main dining room. We'll be selling these decadent goodies in the specialty bakeshop instead. But for now, you get to taste the finished product." Annette removed a dish from the fridge and set it on the counter before lifting the lid.

"This looks delicious." Millie's mouth watered as she peered at the individual cheesecakes, topped with an apple crumble.

"There's only one thing left to do." Annette darted to the stove, grabbed a small saucepan and carried it back to the dessert counter. She began drizzling the thick liquid over the top. "We add a touch of caramel sauce and voila!"

"They're almost too pretty to eat."

Annette handed one of the mini cheesecakes to Millie.

"You're not going to try it?"

"I've been sampling these for days now, tweaking the recipe until it was perfect."

"So you're tired of eating cheesecake," Millie teased.

"Yep."

Millie peeled off the wrapper and took a big bite. The cream cheese melted in her mouth. There was a hint of tart from the apple, but the drizzled caramel sweetened it.

"Oh my gosh." Millie rolled her eyes. "You have a home run with these."

"You think so?"

"Absolutely."

They were still chatting when an out of breath Amit returned a short time later. "It is done. I found them. Brody, he was harder to track down, but I did it."

"And?" Annette prompted.

"They will both come. Ten o'clock here in the galley."

"Perfect." Millie clapped her hands. "Cupid better start sharpening his arrow."

"I hope this doesn't backfire on us." Annette followed Millie to the galley door.

"When's the last time one of our plans backfired?" Millie joked. "Don't answer that."

"Speaking of backfiring...have you heard from Sharky about us crashing his date with Swinglana?"

"Svetlana," Millie corrected, "and no. I figured I would give him time to cool off and wait until tomorrow morning to apologize."

"Probably a good idea," Annette agreed. "How's it going with Andy's new employee?"

"He loves her," Millie said. "Me? Not so much."

"Why?"

"I don't think she likes me."

"Give her a chance to warm up."

"I'm working on it." Millie thanked her friend for coordinating Brody and Danielle's date and stepped into the corridor. It was time to get to work.

Millie spent the next couple of hours completing a thorough inventory and inspection of the areas on her list. After finishing, she decided to swing by Dave Patterson's office to try to find out what had happened on the dock earlier.

Patterson was behind his desk, his eyes focused on his computer screen. He glanced up when Millie rapped lightly and then did a double take. "Hey, Millie."

"Hi, Patterson. Do you have a minute?"

"For you, I have two."

"I thought I would stop by to see what happened on the dock earlier."

He lifted a brow. "News travels fast."

Millie explained she'd taken Scout to the park and noticed police cars in front of the abandoned warehouse on her way back to the ship. "Johar told me it was a homeless man. I wondered if it was the same one who stopped Cat, Danielle and me last night."

"We believe it is, based on your description. You were on my list to track down, but now that you're here." Patterson grabbed his cell phone, switched it on and then handed it to Millie. "Is this the man?"

Millie slipped her reading glasses on and studied the screen. "It was dark, but yes. This does look like the same man."

"He had some American money in his pants pocket."

"That could be the money we gave him," Millie handed the phone back. "What happened?"

"I don't know the details. He's shaken up but appears to have only minor injuries."

"Someone attacked him?" Millie's heart skipped a beat.

"We believe that may be the case."

"Which means he probably wasn't the man who attacked Nikki."

"Or maybe it was him. It's possible he and the woman who was with him had some sort of argument, and she was the one who injured him."

"True." Millie grew quiet as she mulled over Patterson's information.

"The wheels are spinning," he teased.

"They are. Something isn't adding up."

"We've questioned other area port security personnel and..." Patterson abruptly stopped.

"And what?" Millie prompted.

"Nikki's attack wasn't the first incident." Patterson explained there had been several random incidents the past couple of weeks involving both cruise ship passengers and crewmembers who had been robbed along the same stretch of the docking area.

"You would think the police would step up patrols," Millie said.

"They have, but from what I was told, the attacker or attackers have somehow managed to stay one step ahead of the authorities. They seem to know when the coast is clear."

"Maybe someone on the inside is helping them," Millie mused.

"Meaning the local authorities." Patterson ran a ragged hand through his hair. "We can't stop anyone from leaving the ship. I hope the authorities will have apprehended the attacker or attackers before the passengers start arriving on Friday."

"Right." Millie absentmindedly stood. "Do you know the man's name?"

"Halbert Pennyman. He's a seventy-two-year-old drifter from nearby Salisbury. He's well-known around these parts. His nickname is Halbert the

Homeless." Patterson's chair squeaked loudly as he leaned back. "I recognize the look on your face. It's best to leave the investigation to the local and port authorities, Millie. We're in uncharted territory."

"I feel bad. He was trying to warn us to be careful, and then he's the one who ends up getting hurt." Despite Patterson's warning, Millie figured it wouldn't hurt to do a little more digging around online.

When she got back to the apartment, Millie scanned her emails and then opened a search screen. Although she'd tried searching earlier, she figured another try with different key words might lead her to new information. Millie typed in "Southampton cruise ship terminal attacks."

She tried several combinations of searches before finally giving up. There was no news about Nikki's attack or the recent incidents Patterson had mentioned.

She closed the search screen and wandered to the door, her eyes drifting to the building where

Pennyman had been found. Patterson mentioned the man was well-known to the locals. Surely, if he was a troublemaker, the authorities would have already picked him up.

Something told Millie that Pennyman was not responsible for Nikki's attack or the other recent incidents. Perhaps it was a rough area, and crimes were a common occurrence.

Millie exited the apartment and headed topside to continue working on her scheduled tasks, mindful to keep an eye on the clock. She checked in with Annette once, to make sure Brody and Danielle's romantic rendezvous was still on.

Close to nine-thirty, Millie began to sweat...literally, and she wondered if perhaps they were making a mistake by butting in. On the one hand, the date could blow up in their faces, but on the other, both had accepted the invitation, believing the other had arranged the dinner. She wondered what would happen once they figured out Annette and she had tricked them.

She hoped they wouldn't be mad and would decide to work through their issues and patch things up...or at the very least, clear the air.

By nine forty-five, Millie's sweaty palms turned into sweating bullets. She almost called Annette for an update but knew her friend would be in the thick of things taking care of the last-minute details.

The women planned to hide out in the back of the empty main dining room, far enough away so that they weren't spying, yet close enough to intervene if the couple started yelling.

Millie reached the dining room and began making her way to table three forty-one near the window, off to the side and out of sight. She could hear metal dishes clanging, and the temptation to scope things out was too great.

She zigzagged past the tables, around the server's station and peeked into the kitchen. Annette darted back and forth from a table to a nearby counter.

A starched white tablecloth covered the small table. A battery-powered candle, with its light flickering brightly, was in the center. A small side table was next to it and stacked high with covered dinner trays.

She watched her friend pour sparkling water into the wine glasses and then take a step back.

"Pssst," Millie hissed.

Annette caught Millie's eye and held up a finger, before turning her attention to the table where she placed two sets of wrapped silverware on each side of the charger plates.

She took a step back to inspect her handiwork. Then, she ran to the light switch and dimmed the lights.

Millie held the dining room door as Annette hurried to join her. "Finished with five minutes to spare."

"It looks so romantic." Millie clasped her hands. "You did an awesome job."

"For a galley kitchen, which is usually filled with hundreds of workers and the scene of pure chaos, I guess I didn't do too badly."

The women grew quiet, their eyes on the corridor entrance.

The door swung open, and heavy footsteps echoed on the gleaming galley floor as the first guest arrived.

Annette elbowed Millie. "Do you see what I see?"

Chapter 11

Millie's heart skipped a beat. "Brody brought flowers."

"Way to go, Brody," Annette whispered back.

The women watched Brody make his way to the table and trays Annette had carefully arranged. He made a small coughing sound and nervously tugged on the sleeve of his button-down shirt.

Millie cupped her hand to Annette's ear. "He's nervous." The last time she'd seen Brody in anything other than his uniform was at her wedding.

"Brody cleans up nicely." Annette pressed both hands to her chest. "If only I were thirty years younger."

A movement near the door caught their attention, and Danielle appeared. She paused for a second before making her way inside.

Brody slowly made his way over, clutching the bouquet of bright flowers. He handed them to Danielle and said something, but Millie couldn't hear what it was. "That's our cue to exit," she mouthed.

Annette made a move to step away from their hiding spot at the same time as Millie. The heel of her shoe caught on the corner of a beverage cart, and she lost her balance, her arms flailing wildly as she tried to recover.

Millie lunged forward in an attempt to steady her friend, but it was too late. Annette's flailing arm made contact with the coffee carafe. She hit it with the edge of her hand, flipping the lid. *Tink.*

The carafe flew off the cart and fell to the floor with a loud *clank.*

Brody appeared in the doorway. "Hello."

"Hey, Brody." Millie snatched the carafe off the floor and quickly set it back on the cart. "Sorry. We were just leaving."

"Carry on." Annette grabbed Millie's arm and dragged her away from the doorway, not slowing until they were out of the dining room and on the other side of the hostess station.

"I can't believe I did that," Annette grimaced. "So much for setting a romantic scene."

"It definitely wasn't a smooth getaway," Millie joked. "We need to find another place to hang out."

"There's a set of cozy couches not far from the coffee bar," Annette suggested.

The women made their way down the long corridor, passing by the side galley entrance. There was a small light coming from within, the electric candle Annette had placed on the intimate table for two.

Annette made her way behind the coffee bar counter and rummaged around in the cupboard until she found a small brew pot. After brewing the coffee, they carried the full mugs to a nearby couch.

"I hope we didn't make a big mistake."

"Millie's Matchmaking 101," Annette teased. "Even if it doesn't work out, at least we tried."

The women talked in hushed tones, keeping an eye on the clock. An hour passed, and then an hour and a half. The women had finished the pot of coffee and returned to the coffee bar to clean up.

Millie consulted the clock again. "Brody has less than half an hour to report to work. I'm sure they're gone by now."

"I'll check." Annette strolled down the corridor. She bounced on her tiptoes, peering in the galley window and then motioned for Millie to join her.

"Well?"

"They're gone." Annette eased the door open and made her way to the corner table. The dirty dishes were stacked neatly on top. She lifted one of the lids. "The good news is they stayed long enough to eat."

Millie lifted the lid on a second dish. "You're right." She pointed to the empty dessert plate with traces of caramel sauce still drizzled along the edge. "And they ate all of your delicious dessert."

"I call this a success." Annette lifted her hand, and the women high fived.

Millie set the top on the counter, and something caught her eye. "What's this?" She lifted a folded sheet of paper. Scrawled on the front was Millie and Annette's name. "They left a note."

She unfolded the note and began to read,

"Dear Matchmakers, aka Annette and Millie,

It didn't take long for Brody and me to figure out YOU TWO were the ones who instigated this date and...thank you. We had a wonderful evening, the food was delicious, the company was good.

Thank you for butting in."

The note was signed, Danielle and Brody.

"Bless their hearts." Millie handed the note to Annette. "They're not mad, and they didn't leave us hanging on how the date ended."

Annette grinned widely. "And they lived happily ever after."

"Hopefully." Millie stifled a yawn. "It's getting late."

"It is." Annette reached for the dirty dishes.

"Let's do this." Millie and Annette made quick work of loading the dishes into the dishwasher and clearing the table. After they finished, Millie waited for her friend to shut the lights off and exit the galley.

Millie took one final look back at the empty table and smiled. Despite the chaos of earlier events, it had turned out to be a good day after all.

*****

Nic was up and out the door early the next morning for another round of staff meetings.

Millie waited for him to leave the apartment before getting ready. Andy's schedule for their last full day before passengers began arriving on Friday was filled with practices, including one for a new "Welcome to the British Isles" show. It was a variation of the "Welcome Aboard Show," complete with bagpipes instead of an orchestra, a mock Scottish swordfight and a scene from the Highlander.

There were also new rounds of trivia focused on the port stops. Because of wet weather around the isles, Andy had ramped up the number of indoor activities.

Before she left the apartment, Millie's boss had sent her a message asking her to meet him on the sky deck to discuss something "important." She arrived promptly at eight to find Andy already waiting, holding a large box and beaming from ear-to-ear.

Millie eyed the box suspiciously. "What's that?"

"A surprise."

"I'm all surprised out," Millie said bluntly. "Besides, your surprises usually involve being zapped or hosting impromptu activities that don't pan out."

"You're turning into such a Negative Nelly." Andy slid the box on top of a nearby table and flipped the flaps. He reached inside, pulled out a plaid piece of material and handed it to her.

"What's this?"

"What does it look like?"

"Clothing." Millie turned it over in her hand.

"It's not just any clothing. It's the modern version of a Highland dress, or at least as close as I could get. This is your new uniform for the summer." Andy eagerly reached inside the box again and pulled out a black velvet blouse. A thin layer of frilly white lace lined the V-neck and hem.

"I want to see how it looks." Andy thrust the garments in her hand before grasping her arm and propelling her toward the nearest women's restroom. "I want you to try it on."

"Now?"

"Yes. I need to order more for Danielle and Sophia if this looks as good as I think it's going to."

"I..."

Andy waved his finger in Millie's face. "No excuses. Hurry up. We don't have much time."

Millie shot him a troubled look before clamping her mouth shut. She slipped into the bathroom and removed her work uniform before pulling on the plaid skirt. She eased the black velvet blouse over her head, tugging hard to get the stretchy material over her chest. It was snug but not uncomfortable.

She pivoted to the side to inspect the outfit in the mirror. It wasn't horrible except for her pasty white legs. Millie's first thought was they reminded her of a Q-tip. Her knees were clearly visible, and she could feel cool air blowing up the bottom. Millie felt half dressed.

She unlocked the bathroom door and stuck her head out. Not only was Andy waiting for her, but also Donovan and Nic, who wore an amused expression.

"There she is." Andy motioned for Millie to join them.

"No way." She tightened her grip on the door handle. "This is embarrassing."

"You're being silly." Andy darted to the door and yanked it open. "C'mon."

"No." Millie stubbornly shook her head.

"Come on, Millie," Nic cajoled. "How bad can the outfit be?"

"This bad." Millie cleared the doorway, a sullen look on her face as she lowered into a small curtsy.

"You look…" Donovan doubled over and burst out laughing. "I'm…I'm sorry, Millie. I don't believe I've ever noticed your knees before."

"No, and you shouldn't be noticing them now." Millie glared at Andy, who ignored the look. He made a twirling motion with his finger. "Turn."

"You've got to be kidding."

"The longer you stand there and argue, the longer you're going to be wearing the outfit."

"Fine." Millie stomped in a circle and then ran back into the bathroom. She slammed the door shut and flipped the lock, all the while mumbling under her breath.

Millie emerged to find Donovan swiping at his eyes. Nic wasn't much better. He attempted to give her a sympathetic smile as his lower lip trembled violently.

"Very funny."

"I'm sorry, Millie. You looked adorable," Nic said.

"Sixty-something women should not look adorable." Millie tossed the garments to Andy. "I'm not wearing these."

"You have to. It's going to be your new uniform."

"Over my dead body," Millie shot back. "Look at these two. They can barely control their laughter."

"You're overreacting."

"No. I'm not." Millie crossed her arms. "The outfit would be perfect if I was in my twenties, but it's not designed for someone my age. In fact, it should come with a warning label saying, "Not suitable for anyone fifty-five and up."

"You hated the outfit that much?" Andy cast a puzzled look at her as he carefully folded the garments and placed them back inside the box.

"I don't hate it. It's just not age-appropriate."

"Even the top?" Andy probed.

"The top was okay. Look at him." Millie pointed at Donovan. "I looked ridiculous."

"What if I told you that you could choose either a longer skirt or a pair of plaid capris instead?" Andy wasn't ready to give up on his vision of a Highland attired staff.

"Capris?" Millie's eyes narrowed. "I...maybe. I would need to try them on first."

"I have a pair in the office."

"Then why didn't I try those on instead?"

"Because I was so sure the skirt would be perfect."

"You thought wrong, at least for me." Millie calmed. "I get the whole outfit theme, but my white legs need some serious tanning before they're gonna be on display."

"But..." Andy said.

Millie lifted a hand. "No buts."

"You heard Millie." Andy turned to Donovan. "The Highland outfits are a go. Do I have your approval to purchase the new uniforms?"

"Yes." Donovan was still smiling. "I approve. Just the look on Millie's face was worth it."

"I think it's a nice addition to our summer theme." Nic smiled at his wife. "You're a good sport. Andy's only trying to give your outfits a new look."

"The top was cute," Millie admitted. "The skirt was too much, though. Is there anything else you're going to surprise me with?"

Nic consulted his watch. "I need to get back to the bridge now that Millie's mini fashion show has ended."

"The outfit is the only reason you came up here?"

"Pure entertainment," Nic teased. He planted a quick kiss on his wife's cheek and headed down the nearby steps.

"You're here for the entertainment factor, as well?" Millie turned to Donovan.

"I'm here to approve the expense and to discuss Sharky," Donovan said.

"What's wrong with Sharky? Did he file a complaint about me? Annette and I were only trying to help him yesterday. We didn't mean to ruin his date."

"It's something we can discuss in a few minutes."

"I need to get going," Andy said. "Stop by my office later, Millie, and I'll let you decide between the longer skirt and the plaid capris."

Millie interrupted. "I'll pick the capris over the skirt all day long. I can't speak for Danielle or the others, but capris for me. I'll stop by later to try them on."

"Got it." Andy gave her a thumbs up. He closed the top of the box and followed Nic, heading down the stairs and out of sight.

"We can talk downstairs in the maintenance area." Donovan began walking.

"This was all a misunderstanding," Millie hurried to keep up. "Annette and I weren't stalking him. We were concerned for his safety."

"I hear what you're saying, Millie. Sharky deserves to tell his side of the story." Donovan held the door and waited for her to step into the crew hall. "He's downstairs waiting for us."

Chapter 12

Not only was Sharky waiting for them in his office, but so was Annette, who sat glaring at the man across from her.

"Thank you for making it down here on such short notice, Annette," Donovan motioned to Millie. "Have a seat."

He waited until Millie was seated before turning his attention to the maintenance supervisor. "Now that we're all here, what is going on?"

"This." Sharky jabbed his finger at Annette and Millie. "These two busybodies stalked me and my girlfriend, Svetlana. They barged in on our date and ruined it."

"We weren't trying to. Annette and I were in the area. We decided to swing by to check on you. We took a quick glance in the window, watched as you left the table and then watched Svetlana swap your drinks."

"Maybe mine tasted better." Sharky's face turned red. "I spent the rest of my day off trying to convince her I wasn't surrounded by kooky employees."

"Kooky employees?" Annette lifted a brow. "Why would your girlfriend think we were employees?"

"I...because I'm the maintenance supervisor. I'm the boss."

"You're not *our* boss," Millie shook her head.

"Don't distract from the issue at hand." Sharky scooched forward in his seat. "My only day off to spend time with Svetlana was ruined by you two."

"I'm sorry, Sharky." Millie touched Annette's arm. "Annette isn't to blame. She was only there because I asked her to tag along after we finished another errand. If anyone is to blame, it's me."

Sharky stared at Millie, and she could tell he was still seething with anger. He turned to Donovan, who stood quietly listening to the exchange. "Well?"

"Well, what?" Donovan shrugged. "Millie apologized. It appears as if it was a big misunderstanding. She thought she was helping a friend."

"At the risk of repeating myself, she ruined my only day off."

"You want more time off?" Donovan asked.

"Yes. That's exactly what I want. More time off and a promise Millie won't come within a city block of me and Svetlana."

Donovan rocked back on his heels. "I get you're upset. You feel Millie and Annette sabotaged your date. You can have the rest of the afternoon off if Reef agrees to cover your shift."

"He will. I already ran it by him," Sharky abruptly stood. "Your apology is accepted, Millie, but I would appreciate it if you would butt out of my business."

Millie could feel her cheeks redden and she nodded. "Done."

Annette was the first to exit Sharky's office. Millie followed her out. Donovan remained behind, and Millie assumed it was so they could discuss the incident without the women around. She waited until they reached the stairs. "He was ticked."

"Yes, he was," Annette agreed. "From here on out, he's on his own with Svetlana."

"Yep. I learned my lesson. Hopefully, she's on the up and up."

"I'm washing my hands of the entire unpleasant incident." Annette brushed the palms of her hands together. "And on that note, the galley is calling."

Millie realized Andy's early fashion show had interrupted her breakfast plans, and her stomach began to grumble. She was in luck. The grill was open for business and serving breakfast. She loaded her plate with scrambled eggs, sausage links and a generous spoonful of mixed fruit before finding a table in the corner overlooking the harbor with a bird's-eye view of the warehouse.

Millie prayed over her food and reached for her coffee. Had she been all wrong about Svetlana? It wouldn't be the first time.

She thought about the comment Sharky had made about his "employees." Had he fibbed to Svetlana and exaggerated about his position on board the ship?

"Hey, there."

Millie turned to find Danielle standing next to her, a plate of food in her hand. "Mind if I join you?"

"Of course not." Millie moved the wrapped silverware on the table. "Sorry about last night."

"You didn't get the note Brody and I left for you?"

"We did, and it was so sweet. I meant about the peeking in on you to make sure you weren't throwing dishes at each other before we took off."

"How can you throw dishes at a man who brings you flowers?"

"True. So you patched things up?" Millie asked hopefully.

"We're working on it." Danielle pointed her fork at her friend. "I appreciate the nudge in getting us back together, but no more matchmaking."

"Believe me. I learned my lesson." She told Danielle about the meeting with Sharky, Donovan and Annette.

Danielle let out a low whistle. "Whew. He must've been ticked."

"That's an understatement. He was furious." Millie mentioned how Sharky had called them his employees.

"He's telling the woman he's your boss?" Danielle laughed.

"That's his story," Millie sighed heavily as she eased a spoonful of soggy scrambled eggs on top of her toast. "I should've left well enough alone. I shouldn't have dragged Annette into it, either. She has her own problems."

"What's wrong with Annette?"

"I..." Millie lowered her gaze. "I shouldn't have said anything. Pretend you never heard it."

"Okay. Forgotten. Any word on who attacked Nikki?"

"No, but I'm sure Patterson is going to be ramping up security around here now that there's been another incident."

"You mean someone else was hurt?"

"Yeah. It happened to Halbert Pennyman. He's the old man who scared us the other night."

"No kidding." Danielle's jaw dropped. "Was it over by that old warehouse? Is he going to be all right?"

Millie briefly filled her in on what had transpired. "I believe he was telling the truth and trying to warn us."

"Poor guy. Speaking of that, I was talking to one of the security guys. He lived in Southampton before joining Siren of the Seas. He mentioned a serial killer nicknamed the Southampton Strangler."

"Southampton Strangler?"

"It's an old cold case. I guess with the recent run-ins in the port area, it made him remember it." Danielle pushed her plate of food to the side. "As a matter of fact, I planned to check it out."

She pulled her cell phone from her pocket and tapped the screen. "This is interesting."

Chapter 13

"The last time the strangler was tied to a local's death was over five years ago." Danielle skimmed over the news story and handed her phone to Millie. "Whoever injured Nikki and the homeless man is definitely not this person."

Millie studied the blurry screen, squinting her eyes as she struggled to read the words. "Patterson thinks Halbert, aka Halbert the Homeless, was the attacker. I think he's wrong."

"I'm with you. The old man seemed harmless. I mean, why stop three women? Unless he was armed, we could easily overpower him."

"I was thinking the same thing." Millie sucked in a breath. "I guess we'll find out soon enough. I mean, if it happens again."

Danielle jerked back as her schedule app buzzed loudly. "This thing!"

"I shut my zapper off."

"I can't. I can't get it to stop. Andy ordered a new one for me, but it hasn't come in yet." Danielle fumbled with the clasp and pulled off the watch. "Speak of the devil...he's requesting my presence down in the dressing room."

"Ha. You're going to see our new uniform."

"What new uniform?"

"The Highland outfit." Millie rolled her eyes. "Andy made me try it on. Donovan was laughing so hard, he almost split his pants. I told Andy I will not be wearing the skirt."

"I don't do skirts."

"Then go with the capris, which is what I did."

Danielle wolfed down her breakfast sandwich and reached for her napkin. "I don't know where he comes up with some of his ideas."

"He has too much time on his hands." Millie glanced around. "Any word on Sophia?"

"She's driving Isla crazy. Where did Andy find this woman?"

"I don't know, but I wish he would return her," Millie joked. "At least we only have to deal with her for the summer."

Danielle's watch zapped again. "Sometimes, that man has no patience." After she left, Millie finished her food and carried her dirty dishes to the bin near the door. She trailed behind Danielle, still stinging from Sharky's anger.

She slowly made her way down the stairs, where she found herself in front of Ocean Treasures. Cat was standing near the window, clipboard in hand.

She gave Millie a quick wave before darting to the door and unlocking it. "Hey, Millie."

"Hi, Cat." Millie motioned to the clipboard. "Working on inventory?"

"Yeah. I'm getting a shipment of shiny new souvenirs for the summer. Donovan wants me to clear out the stuff that hasn't been moving." Cat closed the door behind them. "You okay? You look like you lost your best friend."

"Sharky's date was a disaster, thanks to me. He's furious, and I feel responsible."

"The Russian woman?"

"Yeah. Annette and I swung by their meeting place yesterday so we could check on him. We happened to catch a glimpse of Sharky and the woman in the corner. He got up to use the restroom, and we saw the woman, Svetlana, switch their drinks while he was gone."

"She put something in Sharky's drink?" Cat's jaw dropped. "Did you tell him?"

"We tried. He didn't believe us. He complained to Donovan Sweeney that we were stalking him."

"What did Donovan say?"

"What could he say? Sharky was right. We ruined his date." Millie grabbed a pen from a nearby rack and began twirling it between her fingers. "I still don't trust that woman. She was up to no good."

"Are you sure you're not making a mystery out of nothing?" Cat teased.

"No. Maybe. I know one thing for certain. I've learned my lesson." Millie dropped the pen back inside the bin. "I better let you get back to work." She exited the gift shop and wandered aimlessly around the ship.

When she reached an upper deck, Millie slowed as she studied the docking area and what appeared to be an abandoned pier. Worn posts jutted at odd angles. The dilapidated dock was missing several boards. She'd heard the pier was the one used by the Titanic when it set sail for Ireland, to begin her final, fateful journey.

Millie wasn't sure if it was true. She'd read up on the Titanic Museum in Belfast. It was on her to-see list. A melancholy sadness filled her at the thought of the tragic sailing and the staggering number of deaths at sea.

She slowly made her way back inside and consulted her scheduler app for her next task. The rest of the day flew by as Millie worked through her new routine, familiarizing herself with areas of the ship she rarely visited.

Evening arrived, and she headed home. The apartment was quiet. With nothing to do, she sprawled out on the living room sofa. Scout curled up on her lap, and they both took a nap, which is where Nic found them when he arrived home later.

Scout heard him first. He leaped onto the floor and ran to the door.

Millie struggled to a sitting position. "What time is it?"

"Time to call it a day." Nic leaned over and kissed her forehead. "Busy evening?"

"No. I'm bored out of my mind. Scout and I were watching television and fell asleep."

"Tomorrow night will be a whole new ballgame." Nic unbuttoned his jacket and hung it on the back of the dining room chair.

"I can't wait. I'm ready for the new itinerary and new passengers." Millie stretched, lifting both hands above her head. "And on that note, I'm ready to head to bed."

It didn't take long for the couple to take turns getting ready. After crawling into bed, they discussed Halbert the Homeless's attack.

"Patterson thinks Halbert and another person, a woman, argued, and Halbert was injured during the altercation."

"He told me the same thing. Regardless of the circumstances, he's an old man." Millie snuggled next to her husband as they said their evening prayers.

They chatted for a few more moments before Millie rolled over. As she drifted off to sleep, she wondered if Sharky and Svetlana had patched things up.

*****

Millie was awake before Nic. She quietly slipped out of bed and tiptoed to the bathroom. By the time she emerged, the bed was made, and the room empty. She grabbed her jacket and darted down the stairs, where she found Nic and Scout on the balcony.

"I'm sorry I hogged the upstairs bathroom."

"I don't mind using the one downstairs."

"It's going to be a beautiful day." Millie slipped in next to her husband and breathed in the fresh sea air. The skies were clear, and the air crisp and cool. "I can't wait for the passengers to start arriving."

"One more day in port, and then we sail out of here tomorrow afternoon."

Millie shifted slightly to face her husband. "Only this once, right? I mean, we're not going to sit in port for twenty-four hours every time we return."

"No. Our schedule will be similar to the one in Miami. The only reason for the change is because we have a final inspection by the local port health authorities before they release us for our summer voyages."

Nic downed the last of his coffee, and Millie followed him into the kitchen. She gave him a quick hug. "Have a nice morning."

"My whole day is crammed full of meetings."

"Yuck. Better you than me." Millie wasn't far behind and exited the apartment, descending several flights of stairs to Andy's office to check in. She could hear the tinkle of a woman's laughter. Through the crack in the door, she spotted Andy and Sophia seated next to each other, their heads close together.

She slowly backed away and tiptoed off the stage, deciding to consult her scheduling app instead and realized she had a meeting with Camille Bessette, the spa manager, and the spa staff to go over the new VIP products and services.

The spa staff was already there when Millie arrived. She slipped into an empty seat near the back.

"Thank you for joining me for this morning's meeting. We have some exciting new products and services for our passengers I'm excited to share with you."

Millie struggled to pay attention as Camille droned on. Finally, the meeting ended. She made her way to the front, where the spa manager greeted her. "Good morning, Millie. I'm surprised to see you."

"You were on my schedule."

Camille shook her head. "Andy called me yesterday to tell me Sophia would be hosting the VIP events."

Millie frowned. "Sophia is working as our in-house shore excursions expert."

"It appears he decided to give her the Diamond Elite's VIP Pampering Party as well." Camille smiled. "I met her yesterday when she stopped by for some treatments. Have you noticed how flawless and supple her skin is? She would be a perfect spokesperson for our spa products."

"I hadn't noticed." Millie absentmindedly pressed a hand to her cheek. "Well, I guess I better get with Andy to find out what's going on." She turned to go.

"Wait!" Camille stopped her. "While you're here, I'm looking for feedback on a new spa treatment I plan to implement. I recently learned about it while on my break and during a visit to a top-notch spa in Scottsdale, Arizona."

"A spa treatment?"

"It won't take long. I promise. We can do a half session. It will take less than half an hour."

"I don't know…"

"Great. You're always such a good sport." Camille nudged her toward the changing rooms. "The robes are in the closet. I'll meet you in treatment room two."

Millie started to protest and then changed her mind. At least someone still wanted and needed her.

The changing room was empty. Millie slipped out of her uniform and into the fluffy white robe. She placed her belongings inside a locker and stepped into the hall. On the other side were the treatment rooms.

She eased the door open. The lights were dimmed, and the faint aroma of lotus flower lingered in the air. Somewhere behind a palm tree echoed the soothing sounds of waves crashing on a beach.

"C'mon in." Camille, who stood off to the side, began wheeling a cart toward the treatment table as Millie crossed the room. "I think you're going to love the cupping treatment. I've done it several times myself. You won't believe how energized and alive it makes you feel."

The small glass globes on top of Camille's cart rattled as she eased it alongside the table.

Millie eyed the globes suspiciously. "What are those?"

"The cups are part of your treatment. I'll explain the process as we go along."

Millie reluctantly climbed onto the table. "Where do you want me?"

"You'll need to loosen the robe and then lie flat on your stomach."

Camille waited for her to roll over and then replaced Millie's robe with a thin sheet. "This is actually a Chinese medicine tradition and becoming quite popular with celebrities."

A blistering heat shot through Millie's lower back and she winced. "What... was that?"

"The cup is heated. Once it's placed on the skin, it creates a vacuum. The cup's suction shifts the body's energy, or Qi, in order to increase circulation, promote healing and relieve pain as well as reduce the appearance of cellulite."

"I could use some of that." Millie forced herself to relax.

Camille glided the cup down her back and then placed another one on her thigh.

She stiffened at the intense heat. "Ouch."

"You really need to focus on relaxing," Camille said.

"I'm trying, but the cups are hot."

"They are? I may have gotten them a little too warm." Camille removed the cups and the glass rattled. "We'll try these instead." She placed two more cups on Millie, this time on top of her shoulders. "How's that?"

"A little better."

The treatment continued as Camille repositioned the cups along her middle back and her thighs. "We're almost done."

"So how's this supposed to work? You mentioned that it increases circulation."

"It does. The heated cups start to cool. It creates a vacuum and works by pulling the toxins from your body." Camille removed the final cup. "All done."

Millie shifted slightly, her lower back twinging from being stuck in the same position. She slowly sat upright, wrapping the sheet around her body.

"Here's your robe." Camille handed Millie the robe, and she slipped it on. "Well? Give me your honest feedback."

"It was...interesting. The first few cups were too hot. The second set was much better." Millie snaked a hand around to her back. "I can still feel a little burning."

Camille leaned in. "There's a small red mark. It was where I placed one of the first cups and it may have been a little too warm. Overall, how are you feeling?"

"I don't feel any different," Millie answered honestly. "The soft music and aromatherapy are nice touches."

"I see." Camille's face fell. "I guess I need a little more practice."

"Practice makes perfect. I'm sure the passengers will love it once you have it perfected." Millie slid off the treatment table and began making her way toward the door.

Camille hurried after her. "Thank you for helping me, Millie."

"You're welcome."

She opened the door to let her out. "Oh...one more thing I forgot to mention. Because the cups pull the toxins to the surface you may notice some skin discoloration or minor bruising for a day or two."

"Seriously?" Millie's eyes widened. "And people pay for this?"

Camille straightened her back. "It's a very effective way to remove toxins."

"Just out of curiosity, how much will you charge for this toxin treatment?"

"A hundred and ninety-five dollars for a fifty-minute session."

Millie let out a low whistle. "Instead of cupping treatment you should call it pay for pain."

"I...I hope it wasn't that bad."

"I'm joking. It wasn't." Millie patted Camille's arm. "Seriously, I think with a little more practice, clients will enjoy the new treatment as much as they do all of the others." She traipsed into the women's changing area.

Millie made a beeline for the large mirror and slipped the robe off, turning so that her backside was facing it. There were several circular red welts clearly visible on her shoulders.

She lifted her leg and peered at the back of her upper thigh where another welt, this one darker than the others, was beginning to form. "Good grief."

Millie dropped the robe in the laundry basket and changed back into her uniform. When she reached the front desk, Camille was waiting for her. "Thanks again, Millie. You were a good sport about letting me practice on you."

"Did she burn you?" the girl behind the counter asked.

"A little. I think I'm gonna have a couple of bruises, too."

"You're lucky. I was Camille's first guinea pig. She got me good. I had red marks on my rear end for a week."

"I didn't heat the cups up nearly as hot as what I had for you, Tina."

A thought popped into Millie's head. "I think you should try the cupping treatment on Sophia."

"You think so? She seems a little..." Camille's voice trailed off.

"Difficult?" Millie prompted.

"More like particular, although she was pleasant enough. We're going to miss you, Millie." Camille snatched a handful of discount cards off the counter and handed them to her. "Would you mind taking some discount cards for your bingo and trivia contests?"

"Of course not. I'll be happy to hand them out. Good luck with Sophia." Millie pivoted on her heel and with a final smile to Camille and Tina behind the desk, she wandered out of the spa area, wondering what else Andy had taken from her and given to Sophia without her knowledge.

She used the nearest set of side stairs to reach the crewmember's galley and the buffet area. Millie grabbed some food and a cup of coffee before heading to an empty table.

She unwrapped her silverware, thinking about how Sophia had been cozying up to Andy...or "Andrew" as she called him. The woman seemed determined to cast Millie in a bad light. She was also beginning to suspect she was secretly trying to aggravate her, but why?

Did Sophia feel threatened by Millie? Was Andy the reason? Whatever it was, she vowed to be on her guard whenever the woman was around.

Millie spotted Annette joining the food line. She sprang from her chair and darted across the room. "Hey, Annette. Are you taking a break?"

"I am. Where are you?"

Millie motioned to her table. "Over by the wall."

"Be right there."

Millie returned to her chair, and Annette joined her moments later. "You ready for today?"

"Yes. I'm bored out of my mind," Millie joked. Her expression sobered. "How are you feeling?"

"Fit as a fiddle."

"Really?" Millie eyed her friend doubtfully.

"Okay, as fit as can be expected. I'm trying not to stress myself out as much," Annette confessed.

"It'll be tough once the passengers board, and it's all systems go."

"I'm working on some stress relieving techniques."

"Like what? I could use a few myself," Millie said.

"Exercise. I'm trying to hit the gym before I start work. You wouldn't believe how quiet the employee workout room is at five in the morning. Speaking of working out, I think Brody and Danielle's date was a huge success."

"It was. I already talked to Danielle, and she thanked us again."

"Brody thanked me, too. Instead of showing up in the galley for his dozen Friday morning donuts, he showed up in the gym to work out after finishing his night shift."

"To get all buff?" Millie chuckled.

"Hey. It's better to lift weights than a dozen donuts."

"True. Maybe I should start an exercise routine, although my million stair steps a day is good exercise."

"I'm also focusing on being better organized." Annette lifted her glass of orange juice. "And cutting down on caffeine."

"Like last night?" Millie chuckled as she remembered the pot of coffee the women drank while waiting for Danielle and Brody to finish their dinner date.

"The coffee was decaf."

"It was?" Millie lifted a brow.

"Yep. I've got a secret recipe for making it taste almost as good as the caffeinated kind."

"I couldn't tell the difference." Millie shifted. "Today will be a big day. I'm worried about you. I've been praying. In fact, it wouldn't hurt if we prayed now."

"You're right."

The women bowed their heads, and Millie prayed for Annette's health. She prayed for safe voyages for Siren of the Seas. She prayed for Halbert the Homeless and ended it with a prayer of thanks for their blessings.

Millie lifted her head as Annette swiped at her eyes. "Thanks, Millie."

"You're welcome. I love you. You're my best friend, and I don't want anything to happen to you."

"All this love in the air is making me sappy." Annette's hand trembled as she reached for her fork. "I'm surprised you didn't pray for Sharky, too."

"That he wouldn't stay mad at us forever?" Millie joked.

"No." Annette shook her head. "You haven't heard?"

Chapter 14

"Heard what?" Millie asked.

"Sharky never returned to the ship last night."

Millie's fork slipped out of her hand. "You're kidding."

"Nope. Sharky is M-I-A. Amit heard from one of the maintenance guys that he was scheduled to start his shift at six, and he never showed up." Annette continued. "They checked the gangway records. He exited the ship yesterday but never got back on. Patterson already searched his cabin. There's no sign of him anywhere. He's not answering his cell phone or radio."

"I..." Millie blinked rapidly, attempting to digest the disturbing news. "Maybe he quit."

"Him quitting was my first thought, too." Annette shrugged. "You can talk to Reef. I'm sure he has more information."

Millie rubbed her chin thoughtfully; certain she'd been right all along to be suspicious of Svetlana. The woman was up to no good. Call it women's intuition or her fine-tuned sleuthing instinct, but something about her had triggered warning bells. "Are...they going to look for him?"

"I don't know. What I do know is that I've washed my hands of the whole thing. We tried to warn him. He not only ignored us but reported us to Donovan. He's on his own."

Their conversation drifted to the passengers who would be boarding later that day, but all the while, in the back of Millie's mind, she couldn't stop thinking about Sharky. True, he had not only reported them, but also outright accused the women of stalking him and told Millie to mind her own business.

It was possible he'd decided to walk away from his job, but Millie didn't believe it. Sharky loved Siren of the Seas. He loved his job. No...something was terribly wrong. She needed to talk to Reef.

Annette wolfed down her food and pushed her chair back. "I hate to eat and run, but I'm on my way to a staff meeting. It's all hands on deck today."

Millie cast a concerned look at her friend. "Please promise me you'll take care of yourself. There's only one Annette, and I hate to see you work yourself into an emergency room."

"I will." Annette stacked her dirty dishes. "Amit is all over me to take it easy."

"Good." Millie watched her friend leave, offering up another prayer for her health. After finishing her breakfast, she dumped her dishes in the bin near the door.

She still had some free time before going over the final details of the private Welcome Aboard gathering for the diamond passengers, something Andy was rolling out for a summer test run.

The invitation-only party involved a champagne toast, unique logoed goodies, raffles for shore excursions, a complimentary chef's table dinner for two and VIP ship tours. Andy had even convinced Nic to allow the VIPs to tour the bridge and captain's quarters, something Majestic Cruise Lines had discontinued years ago amid safety concerns.

Millie's first thought was to track down Reef to find out what he knew, but after yesterday's lecture to mind her own business, she figured she should start with Donovan Sweeney instead.

She made her way behind the guest services desk, and when she reached Donovan's office, his door was shut. Millie gave it a tentative knock and heard a muffled reply. She eased the door open and stuck her head around the corner.

Donovan and Reef were inside. "Millie Armati. Were your ears ringing? I was getting ready to call you."

"I spoke with Annette. She said something about Sharky not reporting to work this morning and figured I would stop by to see what happened."

"Annette is on her way here. Since you two met this Svetlana person, I want to go over the details of what you've seen and heard."

Dave Patterson appeared in the doorway, and Millie shifted to the side to make room. "Thanks for getting here so fast, Dave." Donovan motioned him to join them. Annette followed him in.

"Maybe we should've planned a bigger meeting space," Annette quipped.

"Please close the door behind you."

"Sure thing." Annette closed the door and joined Millie in the corner. "I take it we're here to discuss Sharky's disappearance."

"We are. I'll let Reef start."

"I was telling Donovan about Sharky sending Svetlana money. He has been for weeks now. Right before we got here, he got really secretive. He had been yapping about Svetlana all of the time, and then he just stopped."

"Have you met Svetlana?" Patterson asked Reef.

"Nope. Sharky showed me a picture of her, though." Reef let out a low whistle. "She's a real looker."

"The woman Sharky showed you and the woman he met were not the same person," Millie said bluntly.

Reef's jaw dropped. "He got catfished?"

"It's possible, although I only saw Svetlana's picture once." Millie repeated the story of how Annette and she had stopped by the Cork & Olive to check on Sharky.

Annette picked up. "He left to go to the bathroom. While he was gone, Svetlana swapped their drinks. We knew we needed to confront her and tell Sharky what she'd done. While we were telling him about the drink switcheroo, Svetlana stormed out, and Sharky chased after her. Next thing I know, we're getting called onto the carpet, with him complaining we were butting into his business and stalking him."

"For the record, I believe Svetlana has something to do with Sharky's disappearance," Millie said.

"We don't know if he disappeared or if he walked off the job," Donovan pointed out. "Which is why you're here. He isn't answering his radio or his cell phone. Patterson and I hoped you might have some additional information about the woman."

"Woman may not be the correct term," Annette said. "The point is debatable."

"You don't think she's a woman?" Donovan looked incredulous.

"Annette and I both agree she possessed some...male mannerisms."

"Including a set of hairy legs," Annette added. "Of course, some European women don't shave their legs and underarms. I give it a 50/50."

"Au natural. It's more of a French thing, I think." A sudden thought popped into Millie's head. "Did you check the abandoned warehouse? Maybe Sharky was on his way back late last night, and he was attacked."

"The warehouse is clean," Patterson said. "We checked all along the dock area and with the other ship's port security as well. No one we spoke to has seen Sharky."

"What about his cabin?" Annette asked.

"All of his belongings are still there."

"Like he was coming back," Millie whispered. "This is terrible."

"Can you think of anything else Sharky or Svetlana said or did, which may have struck you as odd," Patterson probed.

"No. He was ticked off. I think he was fibbing to Svetlana, giving her the impression Annette and I were his employees."

"You're right. I remember him saying something about that yesterday during our meeting," Donovan said.

"Well..." Annette shrugged. "I've told you everything I know. I hope you find Sharky, but at this point, I'm going to do what he asked and butt out."

"I appreciate your time, Annette," Patterson turned to Millie. "You're free to go, too, unless you have something to add."

"No." Millie reluctantly followed Annette out of Donovan's office. "I think something is terribly wrong. Sharky loves his job. He would never not show up. This Russian woman...man...whoever has done something to him." An even more horrifying thought occurred to Millie. "What if he was on his way back here, he was robbed and then tossed into the water?"

"It's a stretch." Annette tapped her lower lip. "Possible, I suppose, but still a stretch."

"It wouldn't hurt for us to have a look around."

"Us?" Annette shook her head. "The ship's crew has already searched the port area. Besides, we made a promise. We promised to mind our own business, which is exactly what I intend to do."

"Annette..." Millie gave her a pleading look. "What if he's hurt? What if he's dying in a ditch somewhere?"

"Then my face won't be the last thing he sees before he meets his maker."

"That's harsh," Millie chided. "I would search for you if you were missing."

"And I would search for you."

Millie frowned.

"Stop." Annette briefly closed her eyes and sucked in a breath. "I...okay. We can have a quick look around the harbor area, but I'm warning you now a quick search is the extent of it. I've spent more time trying to keep Sharky out of trouble than I have my own self."

"I knew I could count on you." Millie clutched Annette's arm. "It won't take long. We'll take a quick look around and come back. At least we'll know we tried."

"Let me give Amit a heads up before I come to my senses." Annette unclipped her radio from her belt. "Amit, do you copy?"

"Go ahead, Miss Annette."

"Millie and I are going to run a quick errand. Can you cover the galley for about an hour?"

"Yes, of course."

Annette thanked Amit and clipped the radio to her belt. "Do you need to clear it with Andy?"

"Nope." Millie consulted her scheduling app. "We're hosting a VIP Welcome Aboard show later. Of course, I'll have to be on hand to greet the passengers, but I still have most of the day."

The women headed for the nearest set of stairs and the crewmember's gangway.

Millie and Annette dinged their keycards before turning left toward the main port area. They showed their identification to the guard on duty and passed through the checkpoint before turning left again, in the direction of the warehouse and other cruise ship docks.

Siren of the Seas was one of only two ships in port, which made the ship's crew even more of a target.

Perhaps Svetlana wasn't responsible for Sharky not showing up for work. The fact they'd witnessed the woman switch out the drinks was concerning. Millie slowed. "What if the dock area attacker and Svetlana are working together?"

"I hadn't thought of that," Annette said. "As much as I'm concerned about Sharky, he should've listened to us when we tried to warn him."

"No doubt, but the man is stubborn as a mule and blindsided by his infatuation with this woman...person. Svetlana."

They hurried past the abandoned warehouse where Halbert Pennyman had been found, and Millie wondered how he was doing. They cleared the area and continued at a fast clip until they reached a marina where several small sailboats were docked.

"Let's start here." The women slowly wandered to the end of the first dock. Millie's eyes skimmed the water for floating objects.

They retraced their steps before walking to the end of the second pier, where the sailboat "Seas the Day" was tied up.

"Cool name. This sailboat looks occupied." Annette cupped her hands to her mouth. "Hello?"

A man emerged from the boat's cuddy cabin. "Can I help you?"

"Maybe." Annette stepped forward. "We work on board Siren of the Seas cruise ship. We're looking for a friend who's gone missing."

"Already had some officers from the ship come 'round a short time ago. Looking for a bloke named Sharky. About yay tall and with spiked hair, like a shark fin."

"That's him," Millie said. "You haven't seen him?"

"No. I've been here for a couple of days and would remember the man. I got a number for someone named Patterson, to let him know if I see him." The man shaded his eyes. "Been coming here on and off for a decade now. Never seen as much trouble around here as this year."

"You're talking about the recent attacks over by the old warehouse," Millie said.

"Aye. I was beginning to think it might be the work of the Southampton Strangler."

"Southampton Strangler," Millie repeated. "I heard about him...her."

"Been years since the strangler's last victim was found." The man shifted his feet. "Didn't mean to scare you ladies, but you can never be too careful."

"You're right." Annette thanked the man, and they continued walking to the end of the pier. The women finished checking the area and returned to the ship, no closer to figuring out what had happened to Sharky than when they'd left.

An uneasiness settled in the pit of Millie's stomach as a wave of guilt washed over her. What if Annette and she hadn't confronted him and Svetlana and accused her of tampering with his drink?

Perhaps he would've shared details about his date, and they could've gleaned more clues about her.

Annette headed upstairs while Millie decided to check in with Andy. She ran into Danielle in the hall outside the theater.

"Hey, Millie."

"Hi, Danielle. Are you ready for today?"

"Yeah. Good thing we're getting an early start. Andy is on a roll. It's going to be all systems go by this evening."

"I can't wait." Millie changed the subject. "Did you hear about Sharky?"

"No. What did he do this time?"

"He's missing."

"Missing?" Danielle's eyes grew wide.

"He never showed up for his shift."

"Maybe he was attacked, too."

"I don't know." Millie swallowed hard at the vision of an injured Sharky. "Patterson seems to think he walked off the job."

"That's crazy. Sharky loves his job."

"That's exactly what I said. Maybe I'll get off the ship again and head back to the place where Sharky met Svetlana to see if they know anything."

"If he did walk off the job, he'd better watch it, or he'll find his stuff sitting on the dock and the ship long gone." Danielle nodded in the direction of the theater. "Andy put me in charge of the music playlist for this week's Singles Mingle."

"Sounds like fun," Millie teased.

"At least I don't have to babysit Sophia."

Millie remembered catching Sophia and Andy in his office early that morning, their heads close together. "I think Andy likes Sophia."

"Like-like?"

"Yeah. Like she's flirting with him, and he's liking it."

"She wouldn't be my cup of tea. Too high maintenance, but then maybe Andy's attracted to high maintenance women," Danielle said. "Speaking of Andy, a word of warning if you're heading that way, I would steer clear of him. He's in an awful mood."

"Why?"

Before Danielle could answer, Andy's booming voice carried into the hallway. "Millie Armati, I've been looking for you."

Chapter 15

"Good luck," Danielle whispered in her ear before hurrying away.

Millie inwardly cringed as she slowly turned. "Hey, Andy."

"Why haven't you called me back?"

"Called?" Millie pulled her cell phone from her pocket. "I don't see where I missed a call."

"I also sent a notification to your scheduler app."

Millie consulted the scheduler. "I guess I must've missed that one."

Andy waved dismissively. "What's the big idea?"

"Big idea?"

"Sophia said you were up in the spa area telling the employees you were in charge of the VIP pampering parties."

Millie could feel a slow anger build inside her, and she clenched her fists. "I went up there earlier to check in because it was on my schedule. I had no idea you turned the VIP pampering parties over to Sophia," she replied in a tight voice. "I heard it from Camille."

"I told you I was assigning some of your jobs to her." Andy calmed slightly. "We talked about it yesterday."

"We did not," Millie argued. "This morning was the first I heard."

"I guess I forgot." Andy fumbled inside his pocket and pulled out a sheet of paper. He handed it to Millie. "Did I give you a copy of this?"

Millie glanced at the paper. "No."

"Are you sure?"

"Positive. What is this?"

"It's the list of tasks I've assigned to Sophia while she's with us. I guess I forgot."

"Maybe because she's got you wrapped around her little finger," Millie mumbled under her breath.

"What did you say?"

"Nothing. Fine. She has the VIP pampering parties. I need a copy of this, so I don't keep stepping on Sophia's toes." Millie handed the sheet back to him.

"I wish you would try harder with her. Sophia is new. She's trying and needs help learning the routine."

"She's trying all right."

"Of course, she is." Andy's expression softened. "The VIP issue was a total misunderstanding. I'll explain to Sophia it was my fault for not giving you a heads up."

"Please do so," Millie said coolly. "Is there anything else? Have you given her the Diamond Elite Welcome Aboard party, too?"

"Of course not. I think you're being overly sensitive, Millie." Andy consulted his watch. "I need to get going. I'm meeting with the entertainment staff to make a few changes to the headliner shows. Sophia is singing a solo tonight. Did you know she has the voice of an angel?"

"I had no idea."

"Wait until you hear her sing." Andy patted Millie's shoulder. "I'll see you later for the Celtic dancer's rehearsal."

"See you later." Millie waited until Andy walked away. "Unless you plan on replacing me with her."

Millie stomped up the stairs to deck seven. The lights to Ocean Treasures blazed brightly. She noticed Cat seated at the desk; her eyes focused on a computer screen and gave the door a quick rap.

Cat's head shot up. She motioned for Millie to hang on as she ran over to unlock the door. "What's up?"

"Hi, Cat. You busy?"

"Not really. I'm updating the last of my inventory."

"I was thinking about running by the place where Sharky met Svetlana to do a little investigating."

"To spy on Sharky again?"

"No. He's missing. He never showed up for work this morning."

"Uh-oh. You want me to go with you?"

"I can always use a second opinion."

Cat glanced at her watch. "I'm finishing up here."

"Awesome." While Cat keyed in the rest of the store's inventory, Millie radioed Andy to let him know she was leaving the ship.

"Where are you going?"

"To run an errand," Millie said.

"Sophia could use a break. Hang on." There was momentary silence on the other end. Andy returned. "Sophia is willing to go with you. When are you leaving?"

"Now. Cat and I are headed to the gangway."

"Perfect," Andy's voice boomed over the radio. "I'll send her right down."

Millie frowned at her radio as she clipped it to her belt. "Great. Sophia is going with us."

"Who is Sophia?"

"Andy's friend. She's a local he hired for the season to help with the excursions." Millie lifted her hands to do air quotes. "She's an expert."

Cat grinned. "I take it you're not a huge fan."

"No, and you'll find out why soon enough. First, I want to stop by the maintenance office to see if I can get my hands on a picture of Sharky. I want to show it to the Cork & Olive bar employees to see if anyone remembers him."

It was a quick trip down the steps to the lower deck. The women found Reef in the ship's recycling center sprawled out beneath a large piece of machinery.

"Reef?"

Reef kicked the dolly forward and rolled out from under the equipment. "Hey, Millie."

"Any word from Sharky?"

"Not a peep."

"Cat and I are heading to the bar, the place where Sharky met Svetlana. I'm hoping you can help me track down a picture of him."

"There's one in the maintenance office." Reef wiped his hands on his work pants and motioned for them to follow him out of the recycle center. "I think Donovan and Patterson plan to write him off, but I know Sharky. Something ain't right."

"I agree." Millie and Cat hurried to keep up with Reef's long paces. "I don't trust that woman...err...person."

"You really think Svetlana is a guy?" Reef shot Millie a sideways glance.

"It's possible. Annette and I both wondered the same thing."

They reached the maintenance office where Reef unlocked the door. He flipped the light switch and strode inside. "Over here."

Millie followed him behind the desk to the filing cabinet. On top of the cabinet was an eight-by-ten picture of Sharky, his hair spiked up, the tips dyed blond and an unlit cigar dangling from his mouth.

"This is perfect." Millie slipped her cell phone from her back pocket, switched it on and snapped a picture.

"I was gonna check around for him later myself after I finish my shift," Reef said.

"I'll let you know if we find anything," Millie thanked him, and she and Cat headed out. The crew gangway was a short walk from the maintenance area.

Sophia was already on the dock waiting - or more like pacing - when Cat and Millie arrived. "I was getting ready to give up on you."

"We had a small errand to run first," Millie greeted her coolly and motioned to Cat. "This is my friend, Cat. She manages the ship's main gift shop, Ocean Treasures."

Cat extended a hand, and Sophia pretended not to see it as she stared at Millie. "Andrew seems to think I'll benefit from spending time with you. It will help us bond," she mocked.

"He's the boss," Millie forced a smile. "Shall we?"

The trio made their way to the end of the pier. They passed through the security checkpoint and paused when they reached the corner.

"Which way?" Cat shaded her eyes.

"This way." Millie turned in the direction of the Cork & Olive. She slowed when she reached the entrance to the bar and peered through the glass door.

"What are we doing here?" Sophia curled her lip. "This is a dive pub."

Millie ignored Sophia's comment as she swung the door open and stepped inside. The place was empty except for a young couple in the corner. She approached the bar and climbed onto a barstool.

Cat joined her while Sophia trailed behind. She tapped Millie on the shoulder. "This is against company policy."

"What are you talking about?"

"Drinking on the job. I'm going to have to report this."

"To who?" Millie chuckled. "The captain?"

"I'm growing weary of all of this faffing about. I'll wait outside while you disregard company policy." Sophia stomped out of the bar.

"What does that mean - faffing about?" Cat asked.

"I have no idea, but I'm pretty sure it wasn't anything good." Millie ignored Sophia, who stood glaring at them through the glass door and spun in a half-circle, facing the bartender.

"Hello. My friend was here the other day. He never showed up for work. I was wondering if you'd seen him."

"What's he look like?" the man asked.

"I have a picture." Millie switched her cell phone on. She pulled up the picture of Sharky and handed the phone to the bartender. "That's him."

The man studied the screen. "Maybe."

"Maybe?" Cat asked.

"This is a bar...a business. Buy something, and maybe my memory will clear."

"Fine." Millie pulled a ten-dollar bill from her front pocket and set it on the bar. "I'll take a Diet Coke." She motioned to Cat. "You want one?"

"Sure."

The bartender glanced over Millie's head. "What about your friend outside?"

"She's not thirsty." Millie watched him pour the sodas. "You can keep the change if it helps your memory."

"Thanks. I made a fifty pence tip," he said sarcastically. "Yeah. I remember the guy. Short chap. Spiked hair. He and a woman with light-colored hair were in here the other day."

"Right. Have you seen them since?"

"Nope. They didn't stay long." The man twirled his finger next to his forehead. "The lady...and I use the term loosely...was a bit lairy. Finally, they left."

"Lairy?" Cat asked.

"You know...loud and brash. We get our share of nutters."

"Nutters?"

"Odd customers. Weirdos." The bartender eyed them curiously. "You're not from around here. You have an accent."

"No. We're not. Not even close. So, you remember seeing our friend and the woman. They didn't stay long. Do you happen to know where they may have been headed?" Millie asked. "I mean, bartenders strike up conversations with customers all of the time. I was hoping they may have said something."

The man shook his head, taking a swipe at the bar with his rag. "Well. Now that you mention it. The woman did say something about staying close by and wondered what our hours were."

"She's staying in a nearby hotel?" Millie's heart skipped a beat. Finally, they might be onto something.

"Or a hostel. There are several on this block."

Sophia returned inside, her face splotchy and red. "Are you almost done? I'm going to pass out from this oppressive heat."

"Yes. We're done." Millie reluctantly slid off the barstool. "Thank you for your time…"

"Kent. You're welcome."

The women exited the bar and stepped onto the sidewalk.

"What was that all about?" Sophia narrowed her eyes.

"We're looking for a friend," Millie patiently explained. "He's gone missing."

"Maybe he doesn't want to be found. Working on a cruise ship isn't for everyone."

Millie didn't reply. There was no sense in arguing with Sophia.

"There's a student food store at uni I want to visit," Sophia said.

"Uni?"

"University. It's more of a co-op. It's a short walk, and the goods are much cheaper than elsewhere."

"Lead the way." Cat and Millie followed Sophia down several blocks before making a sharp right. "We're here."

"We might as well have a look around." Cat headed to the other side of the store while Millie wandered down a center aisle. She stopped when she reached the section of teas and herbs. One, in particular, caught her eye. It was hawthorn berry tea.

Millie picked up the box and scanned the contents. This was the berry Annette was anxious to try. She carried it to the checkout counter, paying cash for her purchase before tucking the tea inside her purse.

Cat joined her and placed her items on the checkout counter.

"Do you have a bag?" the cashier asked.

"Bag?" Cat shook her head.

"For the items. If you don't have a bag, you can buy one."

"Buy a bag for buying groceries."

"Yes. Most people bring their own." The woman offered Cat a tolerant smile.

"I'm sorry. I don't have a bag."

The cashier rang up the purchases and began putting them in a disposable plastic bag. "How much is the bag?" Cat asked as she watched her.

"Fifteen pence."

Millie did a quick conversion. "Just under twenty cents."

"Twenty cents for a plastic grocery bag?" Cat wrinkled her nose. "I guess I'll be keeping it as a souvenir," she joked.

"I always bring my own bags." Sophia, who had come up behind them, began unloading her items on the counter. "It's environmentally responsible to recycle."

Millie watched her pull a cloth bag from her purse. "Perhaps you should remind passengers of the conservation efforts."

"I think I will," Sophia smiled smugly. "Americans certainly do things differently."

Millie clenched her jaw, refusing to take Sophia's bait. She and Cat wandered outside to wait for her to finish paying for her purchases.

"She's a trip," Cat said. "Where did Andy find her?"

"They're old friends. Thankfully, it's only for the summer."

"Better you than me." Cat shifted the bag to her other arm. "What are you going to do about Sharky?"

"I've been thinking about it. First, I'm going to make sure there's no word from him when we get back. If he still hasn't surfaced, I have a plan."

Chapter 16

The first thing Millie did when they reached the ship was to return Sophia to Andy...or Andrew as she insisted on calling him.

Cat went to her cabin to drop off her purchases while Millie ran upstairs to track down Annette and give her the box of tea.

Amit was in the kitchen, but there was no sign of her friend. "Where's Annette?"

"She was not feeling too well. She went to her cabin to take a nap. She will be back soon...by four."

Because it was almost four, Millie decided to hang around to see how her friend was feeling and to give her the tea. Annette arrived a short time later, pale and with dark circles under her eyes.

Millie led her to the dry goods storage room, aka Annette's office. "Are you all right? You look terrible."

"I'm not feeling so great." Annette pressed a light hand to her chest. "My angina is acting up."

"I found this at a local co-op today." Millie handed her the box.

"What is it?" Annette read the name on the front. "Hawthorn berry tea."

"It's not the real deal but as close as I could get. I still plan to try to find the natural berries at Blarney Castle Gardens or somewhere off the ship but figured you could try this in the meantime."

"Thank you. I will. Right now, in fact." Annette carried the box to the counter. She grabbed a teacup from the cupboard, filled it with water and stuck it in the microwave. "Any word on Sharky?"

"No, but we found out something interesting when Cat and I went back to the Cork & Olive." She briefly filled Annette in on what the bartender had told them. "He said there are several hostels around here."

"Hostels are cheaper than staying at a hotel," Annette said. "So, you think he's nearby?"

"That's my guess. If Sharky doesn't show up by tomorrow morning, I'm going to go look for him myself." Millie's app chimed. "More schedule updates. I'll let you get to work."

Annette thanked her again for the tea, and Millie promised to check on her later.

Her next stop was Patterson's office to see if there was any word from Sharky. When Millie arrived, she found the head of security seated at the desk, cell phone in hand and a troubled expression on his face.

"I see. You're sure he saw someone hanging around the abandoned warehouse last night...and a burner barrel." Patterson ran a hand through his hair. "We have one more day to get to the bottom of this before we leave port. I want extra security on the ground tonight."

Patterson abruptly ended the call and tossed his cell phone on the desk.

"More trouble in the dock area?"

"I don't know. Maybe. Just between you and me, the port authorities are reluctant to cooperate with us."

"Because it's bad for business," Millie guessed. "If the news of potential issues hit the papers, passengers might have second thoughts about cruising from here."

"Yes, and they view us as outsiders. The only option is to increase our security presence without stepping on the local authorities' toes." Patterson changed the subject. "To what do I owe the pleasure of your presence?"

"I'm here to see if you've heard from Sharky yet."

Patterson shook his head. "Not a peep. It's as if he dropped off the face of the earth."

"Or is being held against his will."

"He's a grown man, Millie. Maybe he doesn't want to be found."

Millie shifted uneasily. "I don't buy it. Svetlana is bad news. "I'd feel so much better if we could talk to Sharky, to make sure he's okay."

Patterson placed both elbows on his desk. "You're trying to make a mystery out of something that isn't."

"Am I? Don't you think it's odd he just walked off the job? At the very least, he would've taken his things."

"Sharky took some cash from his bank account."

"Locally? Like nearby?"

"Yes. From a convenience store's ATM less than three blocks from here. Sharky is alive and well."

"Maybe it wasn't him."

"Millie…" Patterson warned. "Our guys found out a man matching his description used their store ATM machine last night."

"What if they're wrong? What if it wasn't Sharky?"

"I have other things to worry about…namely the safety of the crew and passengers." Patterson slowly stood. "Is there anything else?"

"No. I have a bad feeling about him."

"You worry too much." He escorted her to the door. "How is your new co-worker working out?"

"Sophia?"

"Andy's friend."

"She's…interesting. Speaking of which, I better head up to the theater. The new Celtic dance troupe is practicing. Andy wants me to be there to give him some feedback."

"I heard about your new uniform." Patterson's eyes twinkled with amusement.

"It's not funny." Millie grimaced. "I can't believe Andy expects us to dress like locals."

"I think it's an excellent way to engage the passengers."

"That's because you're not the one wearing it." Millie exited Patterson's office and climbed the stairs, taking them two at a time.

The sound of bagpipes drifted into the hall. Millie eased the door open and tiptoed down the center aisle. Sophia and Andy were seated in the front row. Millie settled into the seat next to Andy, watching the four male and four female dancers stomp around the stage, twirling and clomping to the beat of the music.

Millie tapped her fingers in rhythm, mesmerized by the lilting notes. The music and dancing ended on a high note.

Andy sprang to his feet and clapped loudly. "Bravo. Well done. An excellent practice run. I love it." He turned to Sophia. "Well?"

Sophia barely made an effort to applaud. "There's room for improvement. A few of the notes were off. The costumes are a little dark."

"I thought they were great," Millie chimed in. "The passengers will love the show."

"You're an expert now?" Sophia shot Millie a look of irritation. The fake smile returned as she touched Andy's arm. "I think with a little more practice, they'll be acceptable, Andrew."

Andy placed a light hand on top of Sophia's. "You're the resident expert."

Millie started to make a gagging sound and stopped herself. "Have you finished picking out the headliners?"

"Yes." Andy cleared his throat as he pulled a folded piece of paper from his pocket. "We have a bang-up line-up. It's one of the best ever." He handed the paper to Millie, and her eyes skimmed the sheet. "It's great, Andy. I think you have a home run with these."

"Thanks, Millie."

"I better get to work before the boss gets onto me for goofing off." Millie headed out of the theater, making her way to the top of the ship and working her way down.

She finished inventorying the supplies for several activities, including the scavenger hunt and trivia games. Up next was checking the bingo balls and making sure there was a sufficient inventory of bingo cards before returning to the apartment.

The thigh burn from the cupping treatment was rubbing on Millie's workpants. She found a bottle of aloe in the downstairs bathroom cabinet and applied a thin layer. She attempted to put some on her back. Unable to reach it, she finally gave up.

She left the aloe on the kitchen counter to remind her to re-apply it later before rummaging through the refrigerator for leftovers. Millie decided on a bowl of gazpacho soup and a turkey sandwich. She placed both on a tray along with a handful of Scout's treats before heading to the balcony.

She set the pup's treats on his mat, poured fresh water from her glass of ice water into his dish and then eased onto a balcony chair.

The loading dock was buzzing with activity. Millie studied a group of maintenance men off to one side. They were pointing at one of the forklifts. Reef joined them. He hopped on the forklift and fired it up.

"I thought I saw you sneak by me." Nic appeared in the doorway.

"I decided to hang out with Scout while I grabbed something to eat." Millie tapped the edge of her plate. "Are you hungry?"

"No. I had a lunch meeting on the bridge." Nic picked Scout up. "Did you leave the bottle of aloe on the kitchen counter?"

"Yeah. It's for my cupping burns." Millie set her plate on the side table and stepped into the apartment. She unbuttoned her shirt and lowered it, revealing the marks on her back.

"What in the world?" Nic gasped. "Have you seen your back? It looks like someone attacked you with a branding iron."

"That's what it felt like," Millie winced as she eased her shirt over her shoulder. "It's a new spa treatment involving hot glass cups. It's supposed to create a vacuum and suck the toxins out of your body."

"Who in their right mind would pay for that?"

"Good question." Millie returned to the balcony where Scout stood sentinel guarding her plate of food. "I bet you wish you could reach that."

Nic followed her out. "Someone has been tampering with the forklifts. Patterson thinks it may be the same person who is harassing the crew."

"Inside the security checkpoint?" Millie scooped up a spoonful of thick, tangy gazpacho.

"No. The forklifts are stored inside a gated area outside the checkpoint."

"Not far from the warehouse," Millie guessed.

"Actually, it's on the other side." Nic shrugged. "Maybe it's a coincidence. This dock area was recently renovated and previously used by freighters, not passenger ships."

"Which means the tampering could have started before we ever got here."

"Right." Nic's radio went off. It was Donovan reminding him of an officer's meeting.

"Duty calls and another round of meetings." Nic gave his wife a quick kiss. "What's on your schedule for the rest of the day?"

"It won't be any more spa treatments," Millie joked. "Seriously, I have some training, more inventory and then later, meeting Andy downstairs to greet the passengers."

"Don't forget to enjoy what's left of your time off." Nic patted Scout's head before heading to the bridge.

With time on her hands, Millie decided to clean the apartment. She turned some music on and started by tackling the huge mound of dirty laundry. It took longer than she anticipated, but when she finished the apartment was sparkling clean.

Thinking Reef might have an update, she ran down to the maintenance office. The office was dark, and the lights were off. She turned to go, nearly colliding with him as he rounded the corner.

They both took a quick step back. "Hey, Millie."

"Hey, Reef. I thought I would stop by to see if there's any word on Sharky."

"No." Reef's shoulders sagged. "Believe it or not, I have even more bad news."

Chapter 17

"Donovan told me if Sharky doesn't show up by the time we leave port tomorrow, he's gonna pack up his things and ship them to the address on his emergency contact information."

"This is terrible."

"I could use him right now. Someone was messing around in the storage area and clipped the wires on a couple of the forklifts."

"Vandals?" Millie asked.

"It's looking that way. What about you? Have you had any luck figuring out what happened to Sharky?"

"The bartender at the Cork & Olive dive bar remembers Sharky and Svetlana. He said she mentioned staying nearby. According to what he told me, there are several hostels in the neighborhood."

"Why would Sharky stay at a hostel? That doesn't make any sense."

"I agree, even if he was madly in love with Svetlana." Millie had a sudden thought. "I wonder if there's some sort of clue in Sharky's cabin."

"Like clues about the Svet lady?"

"Yeah. We could run by there and have a look around."

"Patterson already searched his cabin. Besides, how are we gonna get in?"

Millie tapped the top of her master keycard. "I have a way to get in, but you can't tell anyone."

"My lips are sealed." Reef made a zipping motion across his mouth. "I'll show you where it's at." He lumbered down the hallway, his heavy steps thudding loudly on the concrete floor.

They reached the end of the hall and veered to the left onto another small corridor, one that Millie had never noticed before. The corridor narrowed, forcing them to walk single file. Her heart began to race as her claustrophobia threatened to kick in.

Reef shot her a quick look over his shoulder. "You okay?"

"Yes," Millie gasped. "I'm not good with confined spaces."

"Then you aren't going to like Sharky's cabin." Reef stopped in front of a small door. "This is it."

"You're kidding. It looks like a storage closet. Is your cabin this small, too?" Millie sized Reef up, wondering how the huge, hulking man managed to fit through the door.

"Same size. The upside is we don't have to share, and it's easy to keep clean."

"I suppose." Millie swiped her keycard, waiting for the familiar *click* before she turned the handle and pushed it open. A sour smell emanated from the cabin, and she made a gasping sound as she covered her mouth. "Good grief."

"It's the sewer system. We're down draft of it," Reef explained.

"It's awful."

Reef shrugged. "You get used to it. The light switch is on the right."

Millie flipped the lights on and took a tentative step inside. The interior of the compact space was surprisingly tidy. She took another step, eyeing the cigar case display hanging on the wall.

There was also a cigar-shaped decorative pillow and cigar-shaped wall art above the bed. Sharky's scooter blocked the narrow walkway. "He keeps his scooter in his cabin?"

"Yep. He keeps it locked up in his room when he's not using it because the guys like to mess with him."

Millie remembered the recent banana in the tailpipe incident and grinned. "Yeah. I've witnessed that myself." Her expression sobered. "I guess we'll have a quick look around. You check the bathroom."

Reef nodded as he opened the bathroom door. He turned sideways and sucked in his gut. It was a tight fit as his protruding rotunda rubbed the doorway.

His feet hung over the threshold, and Millie watched him struggle to turn. "How on earth do you shower in there?"

"I don't. I use the showers in the locker room." Reef's voice grew muffled. "Sharky's got plenty of room." The cabinet doors banged shut.

While Reef investigated Sharky's bathroom, Millie turned her attention to the small desk and drawers. She opened the top drawer and peered inside. It was full of snack crackers, candy bars and several cigar boxes.

She closed the drawer and opened the next one. Socks and underwear were neatly arranged inside. Below the drawers was a cabinet. Inside the cabinet was a small refrigerator. It was empty except for two cans of Mountain Dew. She inched to the side and peered into the clothes closet.

T-shirts, black work shirts and matching work pants filled the hangers. Several pairs of black work shoes were below the uniforms, with a pair of tan dress shoes at the very end.

Millie tipped them upside down and gave them a good shake before returning them to their spot. "You find anything?"

"Nope." Reef cautiously squeezed out of the small bathroom. "It's clean."

Millie's next stop was the bunkbed. She pulled the sheets back and lifted the mattress. "Nothing." She placed both hands on her hips and spun in a slow circle.

"I guess this didn't help."

"No. It was a bust." Millie turned to go when she noticed something sticking out of the light bar above the desk. "Hang on." She dragged the cabin's only chair to the edge of the counter and climbed on top.

Millie ran her hand along the edge as balls of dust fluttered down. "Achoo."

"Bless you."

"Thanks." Millie scooted to the side, placing her right hand on the wall for balance and reaching with her left. She grabbed hold of something soft and tightened her grip before carefully pulling it down.

Reef squinted his eyes. "What is it?"

"I don't know." Millie handed him the small notebook and cautiously climbed off the chair.

Reef flipped it open. "Check it out."

Millie slipped her reading glasses on and took the notebook from him. It was full of dates and cryptic descriptions. "It looks like some sort of journal or diary."

"It's a sailor's logbook," Reef said. "Sharky always wanted to join the Navy, but he was too short."

"I didn't know that." She scanned the first page of the notebook with dates from the previous year. Each entry was meticulously written in a series of numbers and words. Sharky had used a coding system for the entries and none of them made sense to her.

"He used some sort of coding system." Millie flipped to the back, and her heart skipped a beat. The last entry was from Tuesday morning. "He entered several notes on Tuesday. I wish I could figure out what they mean."

She pulled her cell phone from her pocket and snapped a picture of the previous week's entries. Millie skimmed several pages to see if Sharky had created a cheat sheet of codes, but there was nothing. "I'm gonna see if I can figure out how to crack the code."

"Why don't you take the notebook with you?" Reef asked.

"What if Sharky shows up? He'll know we were in his cabin."

"True."

Millie climbed back on top of the chair and placed the notebook back where she'd found it. "I have some free time to do a little research."

Reef offered a hand to help her down. "Can I take a look at it again?"

"Sure." Millie handed Reef her cell phone, and he studied the pictures. "Yep. Looks like a secret coding system."

Millie finished a quick search of the rest of Sharky's cabin before they exited into the hall. "Thanks for helping me."

"You're welcome. Do you want to check his locker, too?" Reef asked.

"His locker?"

"The maintenance supervisors each have an assigned locker in the office."

"Absolutely." Millie followed Reef back to the maintenance office and inside, making sure to close the door behind them.

"The lockers are back here." Reef stepped behind the desk and off to the side. He pointed to the locker on the far left. "This one is Sharky's locker."

Millie leaned forward to study the lift latch and large metal padlock. "Are you any good at picking locks?"

"Nope." Reef shook his head. "Wish I was. It would come in handy. Sharky's good at picking them, though."

"I'm not surprised." Millie straightened her back as she studied the lock. "I'm not particularly good at it, either, but I know someone who is."

Chapter 18

Danielle scooted inside the maintenance office where Reef and Millie stood waiting. "Sorry for the delay. I got here as quick as I could. What's the emergency?"

"This." Millie led her to the back of the office and Sharky's locker. "We need you to pick the lock."

"Sharky's locker," Danielle guessed.

"Yep."

"I need a letter opener." Danielle studied the lock. "A set of screwdrivers would work even better."

"Got it." Reef reached behind him and flipped the top on a toolbox. He handed Danielle a set of screwdrivers.

"Thanks. This one should do the trick." Danielle selected a small flathead and inserted the end into the opening before giving it a quick twist.

The lock refused to budge. "Crud. I'll need something else." Danielle's eyes scanned the desk. "A metal paper clip might work."

"We have tons." Reef reached inside the desk's center drawer and handed Danielle a metal clip.

She straightened the clip, broke off a corner section and began twisting it around the end of the screwdriver. "If this doesn't work, we may need a set of bolt cutters."

"Sharky will know we messed with his stuff," Reef said.

"I was kidding." Danielle gingerly turned the screwdriver. The padlock popped, and she removed it from the slot. "Piece of cake."

"You're good," Reef said admiringly. "Maybe you can show me how you did that."

"Later. First, we need to search the locker." Millie swung the door open and began rummaging around inside. Several yellow raincoats hung in a tidy row. A pair of black work boots was at the bottom, and a small toiletry case was on the shelf. The toiletry case contained a toothbrush, travel-size tube of toothpaste, a cheap plastic comb and something Millie couldn't immediately identify. She held it up. "What's this?"

"Hair gel," Reef said. "Sharky goes through it by the gallon."

Millie dropped the bottle of gel inside the bag, zipped it shut and slid it back on the shelf. There was another shelf, this one higher and out of reach. "Is there anything on the upper shelf?"

Reef and Millie traded spots, and Reef ran his hand along the top. "Clean. Nothing here."

"Probably because Sharky can't reach it either. Why don't you search his cabin?" Danielle asked.

"Already did," Millie and Reef said in unison.

"I guess this is a bust." Millie frowned.

"You still have the photos of his journal pages." Reef closed the locker door and snapped the lock in place.

"True." Millie pulled her cell phone from her pocket.

"Sharky has a journal?" Danielle peered over Millie's shoulder.

"Yes. Unfortunately, all of the entries are in code." Millie told Danielle what Reef had said, how Sharky was obsessed with the military.

"Let me have a look." Danielle waited for Millie to pull up the pictures. "This is code."

"Yes." Millie patiently nodded. "It's a secret code."

"It's a hacker code. It's used by computer hackers."

Millie's pulse ticked up a notch. "Is there a way you can crack the code to figure out what Sharky wrote?"

"Possibly." Danielle tapped the screen to enlarge the picture. "I haven't seen this code used in several years. It might take me some time."

"How long? We're running out of time. If we can't figure out what happened to Sharky or he doesn't return to the ship before it leaves port, he's going to get left behind."

"The coded system is on the dark web," Danielle said. "I'll need a computer."

Reef pulled out the office chair. "You can use ours."

"Thanks."

Reef and Millie remained silent as they watched Danielle tap the keyboard. "Great. I can't remember the password." She reached for the mouse.

"Don't give up," Millie urged.

"I won't, but after the third attempt, it will lock me out." Danielle rubbed her hand across her forehead, staring intently at the screen. She snapped her fingers. "That's it. Duh."

She tapped the keys again. "And - we're in."

"How did you..." Reef's voice trailed off.

"You don't want to know, and for the record, you didn't see this," Danielle said.

"Right. Whoa. That's awesome," Reef said excitedly. "Sharky's been trying to hack dark web sites for years."

Millie chuckled. "I'm sure he has."

Reef stared at her reverently, as if seeing Danielle for the first time. "What other cool stuff are you able to access?"

Danielle turned to him, a slow smile spreading across her face. "I could tell you, but then I would have to kill you," she teased.

"Kill me?" Reef swallowed hard. "I...maybe I don't want to know."

She turned her attention back to the screen before shifting her gaze to Millie's cell phone. "I'm assuming you're only interested in the last couple of entries and want me to work my way backward from the most recent."

"Correct," Millie confirmed.

Reef and Millie grew quiet again as Danielle concentrated. She studied the screen and then tapped the keys, going back and forth.

"Any luck?" Millie whispered.

"Yes. Svetlana is referenced several times." Danielle shot Reef a quick look. "You're in here, too."

"I am? What does it say?"

"He said you're sharp as a whip and a great co-manager."

Reef puffed up his chest. "Sharky said that about me?"

"He did." Danielle reached for a yellow pad of paper and pen and began jotting notes. "I think we may be onto something."

Millie leaned in. "What is it?"

"Not what is it, but where is it." Danielle tapped the top of the notepad with the tip of her pen. "He keeps referencing a specific location next to Svetlana's name. It's still in code, but there are enough references you might have something to go on."

"Nearby?"

"Maybe." Danielle pushed the chair back and stared at the screen. "He keeps referencing Itchen."

"Itchen," Millie repeated.

"Let me try an internet search." Danielle opened another search screen. "Itchen is a river. We're only blocks away. The river flows into the port area.

Svetlana and Itchen are mentioned twice. The precise name is River Itchen."

Millie began to pace. "So maybe River Itchen is the area where Svetlana and Sharky are staying."

"That would be my guess. There's one more important clue." Danielle waved the pad of paper. "He's talking about a hostel and a price. Twenty pounds a night, which is pretty cheap."

"What about names?"

"No names, other than Itchen." Danielle squinted her eyes. "There's something else, but I can't figure it out."

She handed the phone to Millie. "You're right. It looks like a bunch of chicken scratch like he was in a hurry. So if we can figure out which hostels are close to River Itchen, we might be able to figure out where Sharky is."

"It's as good a place as any to start," Danielle agreed.

"We need to tell Patterson," Reef said. "This is his deal. Besides, there's still a chance Sharky doesn't want to be found."

"True." Millie plucked her radio from her belt.

"Wait." Danielle scooched out of the chair as she tapped the keys, closing the search screens. "There's a possibility Patterson will recognize the hacker codes if you show him Sharky's journal entries."

"I hadn't thought about that. It could be troublesome for you," Millie said. "And he might wonder how we got our hands on photos of Sharky's journal."

"I could tell Patterson I suddenly remembered Sharky mentioning the River Itchen and a cheap place Svetlana was staying at," Reef suggested.

"Good idea."

"Let me get outta here." Danielle checked the screen again to make sure she'd logged out and then darted to the door. "Good luck finding him."

"Thanks, and thanks for the help," Millie called out, but Danielle was already gone.

"She's cool," Reef said in awe. "Do you think she's a government operative?"

"If she was, she isn't anymore," Millie answered evasively. She knew enough about Danielle's past to know her friend wanted to keep it exactly that...in the past. The fewer crewmembers on board who knew about her previous life, the better.

She radioed Patterson, who told her he would be down shortly, which turned out to be closer to half an hour later. "What's up?"

"Reef and I were discussing Sharky. He may have some new information for you."

Patterson lifted a brow. "You just now remembered something?"

"Sharky mentioned River Itchen. We looked it up, and it's nearby."

"It is. My men have already searched the area," Patterson said.

"What about hostels or hotels?" Millie pressed. "The guy at the Cork & Olive said there are several in this area...cheap places to rent where you can stay off the radar."

"Millie," Patterson said patiently. "Sharky accessed his debit card, which means he's alive and well. We can't go chasing after someone who doesn't want to be found."

"But how do you know that for certain?" Millie pressed. "What if you're wrong? What if they were mistaken?"

"I can't go chasing after every single crewmember who decides they no longer want to work on our ship. All indications are Sharky willingly met with Svetlana, they left the bar together, they met up again and he decided to walk off the job."

"But..."

"I still have my men searching the area, but we can't keep using valuable resources for one crewmember who most likely doesn't want to be found. If Sharky doesn't show up before the ship leaves port tomorrow, then he's lost his job. We pack up his things and send them to the address we have on file."

Millie's heart sank as Patterson gave them both a curt nod and exited the office. She waited for the door to close.

"I'm sorry, Millie. Maybe Patterson is right. Maybe Sharky decided to start a new life here, and he figured it wasn't worth it to come back and get his things."

"But he left his scooter behind. Sharky loves that scooter."

"People change. Maybe Sharky changed."

Millie shot Reef a sad smile and nodded as she trudged out of the office. Maybe they were right. Maybe they were all right and Sharky decided simply to walk away. The ship's staff and crew were not only paid a set salary but were also given free room and board. Perhaps Sharky had been socking his pay away for years, waiting for this day.

Maybe today was the day. With a heavy heart, she returned to the apartment to change into her work uniform. She pushed thoughts of Sharky out of her mind. Soon, the passengers would arrive to embark on their British Isles adventure.

She joined Andy shortly before the arrival of the first passengers, the VIP guests...diamond and then the platinum. By the time the rest of the passengers began boarding, Millie was smiling and soaking up the enthusiasm, reminding herself that not only were many of the passengers embarking on the adventure of a lifetime, but she was too.

She couldn't wait for the second port stop in Cobh / Cork and her planned visit to Blarney Castle. This would be the first castle Millie had ever visited, and she planned to climb to the top and kiss the Blarney Stone to receive the "gift of gab."

Millie flew through her routine, starting with the first round of trivia, followed by the VIP champagne welcome aboard party.

She was on her way to check on the lido deck dance party when Andy radioed her asking her to meet him in his office. Millie could tell from the tone of his voice that something was terribly wrong.

She jogged down the center aisle to the back and could hear loud voices echo across the stage. The office door was open, and Millie stopped in her tracks when she caught a glimpse of the people inside.

It was a solemn-faced Nic, along with Dave Patterson, Donovan Sweeney, Annette, Reef and Andy. Millie said the first thing that popped into her head. "I didn't do it."

"You didn't. Have a seat," Andy said.

"What's going on?"

"This." Patterson unfolded a piece of paper and handed the paper, along with a business card, to Millie.

Chapter 19

"This was delivered to the ship via courier. It was on Donovan's desk when he returned to his office a short time ago."

Millie slowly sank into an empty chair. She slipped her reading glasses on and read the business card aloud:

"Cruise into Love
Majestic Cruise Lines, Inc.
786-229-5220
Sherman "Sharky" Kiveski
President & CEO"

An email address, the cruise line's corporate address and an imprint of a cruise ship with a heart-shaped puff of smoke billowing from the smokestack were below Sharky's "title."

"Sharky created a fake business card listing him as Majestic Cruise Line's CEO?" Millie wrinkled her nose.

"Check out the back," Patterson said.

Millie flipped the card over. Scrawled on the back in black ink was Sharky's signature. "Is this his signature?"

"It is. We matched it to the one we have on file." Donovan rubbed the bottom of his chin. "Read the paper, and you'll find out what happened to him."

Millie set the business card on the desk and began reading the brief note, also aloud:

"Attention Captain of Siren of the Seas,

We are holding your President and CEO, Sherman Kiveski, in an undisclosed location. He is safe and unharmed. In exchange for his return, we require a cash payment of one hundred thousand U.S. dollars in small bills delivered to an undisclosed location by noon tomorrow.

Do not call the police. We are watching you. Another note will be sent via secure email to the ship's captain, Niccolo Armati, at precisely ten a.m. with instructions on where to drop the money. If you fail to deliver said payment as stated, President Kiveski will be killed and his body dumped in the river at our leisure.

Regards,"

There was no signature at the bottom.

Millie's hand shook as she set the ransom note next to the card. "You need to turn this over to the authorities."

"We have. You're holding a copy."

"Sharky created some fake business cards. Somehow, he convinced Svetlana he was president of Majestic Cruise Lines. She met with him, possibly drugged him, which is what Annette and I caught her trying to do the other day, and now she's holding him hostage."

"Again, that appears to be the case. As you read, it appears Svetlana, or whoever she is, has an accomplice."

"Patterson," Millie snapped her fingers. "They mentioned the river. Sharky also mentioned River Itchen. You need to check it out. It's not far from the Cork & Olive where Annette and I saw him and the woman the other day. My guess is they're holed up in a cheap hostel somewhere nearby."

"As I told you earlier, we already searched the river area," Patterson said. "My men are on their way to the local pubs to see if anyone else remembers Sharky."

"We're running out of time. If we don't have the cash to give these people, you heard what they plan to do." Millie's voice raised an octave. "He's fish food, or it may already be too late."

"If they're smart, they'll keep him alive until the last minute to prove they still have him before collecting the ransom money." Nic reached out to touch his wife's arm. "Patterson has contacted the local authorities. They're on the lookout for Sharky. Our men are also looking for him. Perhaps he can convince them he's not who he claimed to be, and they'll let him go."

Millie didn't believe it, and as she studied the faces of the others seated at the table, she knew they didn't believe it either. "He's a goner."

"I'm sorry, Millie," Donovan said quietly. "You tried to warn Sharky. He wouldn't listen. We're doing the best we can. Like Patterson said, everyone is looking for him."

"What if we go through the motions of paying the ransom and flush out the kidnappers?"

Annette, who had so far remained silent, spoke. "The chances of a plan like that being successful are next to nil. It's worth a try, but typically in these instances, the kidnappers use a decoy to grab the goods, throw in a couple of switcheroos and they're gone before anyone's the wiser."

"What about Sharky's email account? He and Svetlana talked for months via the internet. Maybe there's a way to track her down."

"The account was wiped clean," Patterson said. "I suspect Sharky wiped it clean because it contained information he'd given Svetlana - information he didn't want anyone to find."

Millie interrupted. "Perhaps telling her that he was the CEO. Maybe he thought someone might see it, and he would get in trouble."

"A possibility," Patterson agreed. "Or the woman, Svetlana, convinced Sharky to get rid of it before meeting him, so there wasn't a trail. I have someone at corporate working to restore the data, but it could take days."

"I hoped those of you who were among the last to communicate with Sharky would be able to remember something." Patterson abruptly stood, and Nic joined him.

"I told you everything I know," Millie said.

"Same here," Reef said.

"And me," Annette chimed in. "If anyone can survive, Sharky can. He's a wily one."

"If you think of anything - anything at all, please let Patterson know," Andy smiled grimly as he opened the office door to let them out.

Millie followed her husband from the room, and they stood off to the side. "This is terrible."

"It is," Nic agreed.

"Any chance we can delay leaving the port if we can't find him, to buy us more time?"

"You know that's not possible."

Millie knew it would be difficult for Nic to delay the ship's departure. The cruise line incurred hefty fees for every minute they remained in port past their designated departure time.

There were occasions when a cruise line was permitted to remain in port due to a ship arranged excursion returning late, injuries or accidents on board, but she'd never heard of them delaying departure because of a ship's crewmember.

Nic's radio went off. It was Staff Captain Vitale. "I need to return to the bridge." He gave Millie's hand a reassuring squeeze. "Patterson is doing everything in his power to track Sharky down."

"Right." Millie watched her husband exit the backstage and disappear down the side steps.

"Hey." Annette tapped Millie's shoulder. "What do you think about this mess?"

"I think Sharky's in deep trouble."

"Even if the cruise lines were able to pay the ransom, we both know there's no way they're going to do that. But let's suppose they do; the kidnappers can't risk keeping him alive."

"Which means we need to find him as quickly as possible."

"Unless..." Annette stopped.

"Unless he's already dead," Millie finished her friend's sentence.

"Yeah."

The women made their way out of the theater. Millie paused when they reached the stairs. "What about the homeless man, Halbert Pennyman's warning? What if he happened to notice Sharky's kidnappers casing the joint looking for a place to drop the cash?"

"It's possible, and don't forget about Nikki's attack. There may be a link," Annette said.

Millie unclipped her radio and called for Dave Patterson, but there was no answer.

She tried again. Oscar answered Millie's call. "Hey, Millie. Patterson just left the ship. He's meeting his men over by the river."

"River Itchen," Millie said. "When is he coming back?"

"I don't know. Is there something I can help you with?"

"No." Millie thanked him for the information and waved the radio in Annette's direction. "Who knows if, or when, Patterson will have time to try to track down Halbert Pennyman."

Annette shook her head. "We should stay out of this. We've already done enough."

"No. We haven't done enough. I feel somewhat responsible. If we hadn't confronted Sharky and Svetlana, this might never have happened."

"You're wrong. He was gung-ho. You heard Reef."

"What's the harm in making a quick trip to the warehouse to talk to Halbert?" Millie pressed.

"Somewhere in here is a bad idea. I haven't quite put my finger on why."

"Never mind," Millie said. "I'll go alone. Besides, I'm sure you need to get back to work."

"Not yet. Doctor Gundervan is limiting my work hours until I return to the doctor for my test results."

"Did you try the hawthorn berry tea?"

"I did. It seemed to help somewhat. I read the berries in their natural form work much better."

"Which means you're free for a couple of hours."

"I am." Annette grimaced as she consulted her watch. "I can't let you go wandering around abandoned buildings by yourself. Let me go grab my backpack."

"A gun would come in handy right about now."

"Yes, it would. Or even some brawn," Annette said. "I'll meet you by the gangway in ten."

The women parted ways with Millie making a quick trip to the apartment to grab some cash, a flashlight and her taser, just in case. She counted out the cash in small bills, folded them in half and shoved them in her front pants pocket.

She beat Annette to the meeting spot but only waited for a couple of minutes before her friend showed up. She wasn't alone. Reef was with her.

"Reef is coming, too?"

"Like I said, I figured we could use a little brawn."

"And I want to help," Reef said. "Sharky is my friend. We have to at least try to find him."

The trio cleared the gangway area, dodging several stevedores and forklifts who were still loading bins of passenger's luggage.

"This place is a madhouse," Reef said.

"I'm surprised you're not working with Sharky gone."

"I don't have long. I got the next hour covered and was gonna go search for Sharky myself. I was on my way out when I ran into Annette," Reef said.

They passed through the security checkpoint and turned left, heading toward the other cruise ship docks and the small marina. Millie slowed when they reached the entrance to the abandoned warehouse. "This is it."

Reef led the way to the partially open sliding side door. Millie followed behind, and Annette brought up the rear. The interior of the building was dark, with only streaks of light filtering in through grimy shards of broken glass.

"I brought a flashlight." Millie removed her flashlight from her backpack and handed it to Reef.

"This'll help." He turned it on and took a tentative step inside before stopping.

Crunch. There was a faint crunching sound coming from the dark recesses. It was followed by a squeak and a scuttle.

"I saw something move. I think rats are lurking around here." Millie wiggled her toes, anxiously gazing at the cement floor. She tugged her taser from the side pocket of her backpack and pointed it at her shoe.

"You're gonna tase a rat?" Annette laughed.

"Maybe. It depends on how big it is."

Reef cast them a sideways glance. "You two should wait out here until I figure out if the coast is clear." He didn't wait for a reply as he took another step forward and disappeared into the shadows.

His heavy steps echoed from within and then abruptly stopped. Millie strained to hear. "Reef?"

There was a loud *thumping* noise and then a high-pitched scream. It took a second for Millie to realize she was the one who had screamed.

Chapter 20

Millie stumbled backward as the furry critter skittered across the top of her shoe. Thankfully, Annette was right behind her and caught her before she landed on her backside.

"Whoa."

"Something ran across my shoe!"

"It was a mouse. Shh." Annette held a finger to her lips. "Reef's talking to someone."

The voices grew louder.

"Reef?" Millie pushed hard against the metal door, forcing it along the rollers as it made a screeching noise.

Reef stood next to a wooden workbench talking with the man Millie recognized as Halbert

Pennyman. Keeping one eye on the cement floor, she crept inside.

Reef waited until the women got close. "Did I just hear someone scream?"

"It was me. A huge, furry rat this big tried to attack me." Millie spread her hands apart.

"It was not," Annette rolled her eyes. "It was maybe a couple of inches long, and I'm pretty sure he was more afraid of you than you were of him."

"Was he a white albino?" Pennyman asked.

"I have no idea. All I know is he was furry and ferocious."

"He was white," Annette confirmed. "It was a small white mouse."

"That was Gus," the old man said. "He won't hurt you."

"I was telling Mr. Pennyman about Sharky and asking him about strangers lurking around the port area."

The old man eyed Millie closely, his eyes widening as he recognized her. "I remember you from the other night. You gave me some money."

"I did, and I appreciate the warning you gave us. I'm sorry to hear about your attack." Millie studied her surroundings. "Aren't you afraid it will happen again?"

"Nope. I got me some protection. They better not mess with Halbert Pennyman a second time."

"We think whoever attacked you might also be responsible for our missing friend. What do you remember about your attack?" Annette asked.

"They came up on me from out of nowhere and...bam!" Pennyman slapped his hands together. "Next thing I know, I'm flat on my back with a headache."

"Do you remember what they looked like?" Reef asked.

"It was a couple of foreigners. They weren't from around here."

A chill ran down Millie's spine. "Foreigners? How do you know they weren't locals?"

"They talked funny. They speak like dis. Vid out pronouncing certain words."

"Russian," Millie suggested.

"Something like that. The first time they came around, I scared them away, but I'm almost positive they were the same two who came back and conked me on the head. I was telling your friend, here, you need to be careful because they were scoping the place out."

"The ship," Millie prompted.

"The ship, the docking area, the ports, the parks. I seen 'em around," Pennyman pointed to his eyes. "I know who's coming and going."

"Did you report them to the authorities?"

"Every time I report someone, it goes in one ear and out the other. They ignore me because I'm an old man. They think I'm a senile old pensioner, but I know what I see."

"So they didn't believe you when you told them some strange people were hanging around," Annette chimed in.

"Not until I was attacked. I don't think they believed me then, either. They think I fell and hit my head, or a homeless person attacked me, but I know what happened."

Millie shifted her feet. "When's the last time you saw them?"

"Not since the other day. I figured maybe they moved on now that your people have stepped up the patrols around here."

"The cruise ship and port security guards."

"Yes."

"You said there was more than one?"

"A man and a woman. He was kinda tall with short hair and mean eyes. Black eyes like he had no soul."

"And the woman?" Millie prompted.

"It would be hard to forget her. She was a big gal, with some crazy hairdo." Pennyman pressed his hands to the sides of his head. "She had these braided hair saucers stuck to the side of her head and thick bushy eyebrows. She told the man to leave me alone after he knocked me on the ground."

Pennyman told them a security guard riding a golf cart passed by and scared the couple off.

"Any idea which way they went?" Reef asked.

"They crossed over to the other side of the road and then disappeared down a side street. Like I said, they never came back after they attacked me. Good riddance to the riff-raff."

Millie pulled her cell phone from her pocket, clicked on the picture of Sharky and handed it to Pennyman. "Does this man look familiar?"

The old man's eyes squinted. "No. Never seen him before. I would remember his hairdo, too." He handed Millie her phone. "Thank you for the money you gave me the other evening. I bought some food for me and Gus."

A small knot formed in the pit of Millie's stomach as their eyes met. He was the first to turn away. "Little acts of kindness go a long way."

"Like warning three women to stay safe after dark." Millie slid her cell phone inside her backpack and grabbed the fifty pounds in small bills she'd placed in her front pocket. She held them out. "I want you to have this."

Pennyman's lower lip quivered, but he didn't make a move to take the money.

"Go on," Millie said softly. "Take it."

He slowly reached for the folded bills.

"Halbert the Hero who helped save three women from harm."

Annette made a sniffling noise. She reached inside her pocket and pulled out some bills. "I have something for you too."

The old man's eyes shined with unshed tears. "I don't know what to say."

"Promise to never stop caring. That maybe you'll think about getting out of this place...you and Gus...and find a better home with a roof that doesn't leak, somewhere warm and safe."

"We're happy here," Halbert took the money from Annette and shoved that, along with the money Millie had given him, into his pocket. "The guys at the marina, they come around sometimes with food, and I teach them how to fish."

Millie could see Halbert had no plans to leave what he felt was his only "home." "Our ship is leaving tomorrow. Will you be here if we stop back by before we leave?"

"I'm here every day...me and Gus."

"Then I'll be back." Millie gave Halbert the once over. "I think my husband has some clothes that might fit you. You're close to the same size."

"I don't like yellow," Halbert said. "If you got some dark clothes, they don't show as much dirt and stains."

Millie gave him a thumbs up. "I'll see what I can find."

"We better go." Reef eyed the exit. "My guys are gonna wonder what happened to me."

Halbert followed them to the door, stopping just inside. "Thanks again for the money. This will go a long way for me 'n Gus."

"You're welcome." Millie offered him a sad smile, wishing she could do more, but Halbert didn't appear to want help, other than pocket change and maybe some decent clothes. "I'll see you tomorrow."

He gave the trio a small wave and then slipped back inside the dark building.

Reef, Annette and Millie slowly made their way toward the security checkpoint and the cruise ship, a million miles away from the homeless man's shelter.

Reef waited until they were out of earshot. "You almost made me cry back there."

"Me too," Annette said. "What a sad existence."

"It is," Millie agreed. "But you can only help those who want help. Halbert isn't there yet." She grew quiet, making a mental note to check on Halbert each time the cruise ship was in port.

Reef parted ways with Millie and Annette as he returned to the maintenance office. Annette headed to her cabin to change into her work uniform. Millie waited for her in the hall.

She popped out a short time later, and Millie eyed her critically. "Your color looks better."

"I feel better. More like my old self. What do you think of what Halbert said?"

"I think Svetlana - or whoever she is - was scoping out the area with her partner. What are the chances some strangers are hanging around the port, only days before Sharky, aka the president of the cruise line, goes missing, and then someone sends the ship's officers a ransom note?"

"I thought the same thing," Annette said.

Millie followed her up the stairs and to the galley. It was a madhouse with Amit running back and forth. "I better let you get back to work."

"To sit in a chair in the corner." Annette grimaced. "It's driving me nuts."

"Hopefully, it won't be for very long." Millie thanked her friend for accompanying her to talk to Halbert and then quickly made her way out.

It was horrifying to think Sharky had inadvertently set himself up to be kidnapped. It was apparent he felt he needed to fib to Svetlana and tell her he was the president of the cruise lines, even going so far as to have fake business cards printed, just to hold the woman's interest.

If Svetlana was the opportunist Millie suspected she was, she must've started plotting to meet Sharky in Southampton after learning about his position. Could it be Annette and Millie ruined her original plan to lure him to a bar, spike his drink and kidnap him?

Sharky, enraged at them for butting in, had complained to Donovan. In the meantime, he and Svetlana arranged another rendezvous, but before that happened, either Sharky decided he needed to delete any communication hinting he was the cruise line's president...or Svetlana convinced him to delete everything to hide her identity and their possible whereabouts.

The only problem was Annette and Millie had seen the woman at the Cork & Olive. By then, Svetlana and her partner may have already scoped out the port area, picking a location for the money drop.

Halbert had confronted them, and the man attacked him. Now with three eyewitnesses - Halbert, Millie and Annette - Svetlana and her partner needed to speed up their plan.

She thought about Sharky's coded notebook. He mentioned the River Itchen and a hostel. Millie had another thought. She ran down to the security office. Patterson still wasn't back, but Oscar was there.

"Hey, Millie."

"Hi, Oscar. Patterson isn't back yet?"

"Nope."

"Maybe you can help me. You heard about Sharky Kiveski and how he's missing."

"Yes." Oscar nodded.

"Patterson told me Sharky's debit card was used at a local ATM not far from here last night. I was wondering which ATM it was."

"I..." Oscar's eyes slid to a manila file folder on the corner of the desk.

Millie followed his gaze and reached for the file. "Is that Sharky's file?"

Oscar snatched it up. "You know I can't show it to you."

"Can you at least tell me which ATM machine was used?" Millie clasped her hands. "I think I might be onto something."

"Patterson...he will not be happy," Oscar began shaking his head.

"If my hunch is right, I have a general idea where Sharky might be, and it's not far from here."

"Then you must tell Patterson."

"He already knows which is why he's searching the River Itchen area."

"I can't."

Millie switched strategies. "Did Patterson tell you that you couldn't show anyone Sharky's file?"

"No."

She could see from the way Oscar clutched the folder to his chest he had no plans to hand it over to her. "Then maybe you could take a teeny tiny peek inside and tell me the location of the ATM. What you tell me will be between the two of us. I promise."

Oscar scratched the top of his head. "I'll tell you, but you should leave the investigation to Patterson. He's tearing this town apart looking for him."

Millie's heart skipped a beat as she watched Oscar reluctantly flip the folder open. He shuffled some papers to the side and then lifted a single sheet.

"It was an ATM at the corner of Granby and Quarry, three blocks from here." Oscar slammed the folder shut and dropped it on the desk. "Patterson's already searched the area. If Sharky was still there, he would've found him."

"Thanks, Oscar." Millie darted out of the office, never slowing until she reached the apartment. She made a beeline for the computer and let Scout onto the balcony while it booted up.

Millie opened the search screen and typed in Granby and Quarry, Southampton, UK. A description of Southampton appeared. There was a small map to the right of it. She double clicked on the map and zoomed in on the red dot...the intersection of the two city streets. "Well...will you look at that?"

Chapter 21

The location of the red dot, the ATM where Sharky's debit card had been used, was sandwiched between the River Itchen and the Cork & Olive.

Millie studied the map. If Sharky was still alive, he was somewhere nearby, somewhere in the vicinity of the pub, the river and the cruise port.

Annette was probably right. Whoever had Sharky had no intention of releasing him if they got the cash, which wasn't going to happen.

If only he hadn't told the woman that he was someone he wasn't. But then, Millie suspected Svetlana wouldn't have given him the time of the day. Everything pointed to the woman catfishing Sharky, a man she believed was wealthy and worth kidnapping.

Could it be Halbert had encountered Svetlana and her accomplice as they scoped out the area searching for the perfect location for a money drop, somewhere close to the ship?

Millie pushed the chair back and wandered to the balcony doors, her eyes drifting to the marina and the small harbor. The harbor would make an ideal escape route. If someone were to kidnap and hold an important person for ransom, they would want to make a quick getaway.

A sudden thought occurred to Millie. She ran out of the apartment and onto the bridge. Nic was on the outboard deck, talking to one of the ship's officers.

First Officer McMasters was on the bridge. "He shouldn't be long."

"Maybe you can help me. You're English."

"Scottish," McMasters corrected.

"Scottish," Millie repeated. "You're familiar with the Isles."

"I am. It's good to be home."

"I'm curious about the boats and ferries." Millie motioned to the harbor, dotted with small sailboats. "Could you travel from here to say...another country?"

"Aye. The ferry will transport you to a larger ferry port to the south and then across the English Channel to France. The ferry runs every day. It's several hours across to the other side. Are you thinkin' of hoppin' on a ferry?"

"No, but someone else might be." Millie patted the first officer's arm. "You've been most helpful." She ran back inside the apartment and to the balcony.

Millie could almost plot out the kidnapper's plan. Lure Sharky to a meeting spot, drug him, kidnap him and then send a ransom note to the cruise line. The plan would be for the money to be dropped at an undisclosed location close to the harbor in the morning. The kidnappers would grab the cash, and then make a mad dash for the ferry shortly before departure. They could easily be on their way out of the country with cash in hand within minutes.

She returned to the desk and studied the city streets. It was like a big triangle...port to the Cork & Olive to the River Itchen. According to the bar employee, there were several hostels in the area, which Sharky had also mentioned in his coded journal.

Millie needed to check out the hostels, but how? Not only did she need to get into the area hostels, but she needed to do it fast. She consulted her scheduling app to check Danielle's schedule, her first choice for an accomplice.

Unfortunately, Danielle was booked solid for the rest of the day. Up next was Annette. Millie immediately dismissed her. She had her hands full. The last thing Millie needed was for her friend to be thrown into a potentially chaotic situation and stress her heart out even more.

There was also Cat, but the gift shops were open for business. Not to mention Cat was, at best, a reluctant accomplice. Reef would be a good choice, but again, he was working. Millie's schedule app chimed. It was time for her to co-host Sophia's first port chat in the High Seas Art Gallery.

Millie logged off the computer, quickly coaxing Scout back inside and then flew down the stairs. She made it to the port chat with seconds to spare and joined Isla, who stood near the back.

"Hey." Millie slipped in beside her.

"You were summoned here, too?" Isla joked.

"Yeah. Misery loves company." Millie lowered her voice. "How's the new job?"

"Great. I love it. I've been in training for most of the day. Andy wants me to scope out the area after I'm done here, so I have firsthand feet-on-the-ground knowledge for the passengers."

"I thought that was Sophia's job."

"I did too, but it's apparently below her pay grade. She told Andy...or Andrew as she calls him, she wanted to stay on board, getting to know the passengers. Southampton isn't worth her time, so he asked me to have a look around."

As Isla talked, an idea began to form in Millie's mind. She tapped the top of her scheduling app and scrolled the screen, reviewing the rest of her schedule.

There was a break in hosting activities around six. "If you can wait until six, I'll go with you."

"That would be great." Isla was visibly relieved. "Andy told me to buddy up with someone, but everyone else is either practicing for the new shows or scheduled to work."

"I wonder if Andy will let me go with you," Millie wandered off to the side to radio Andy, who gave his approval for her to head ashore. She joined Isla again and whispered the good news.

"Thanks, Millie. I'll owe you one."

"You're in luck. You can pay me back while we're out. I need some help."

Sophia began talking, and she gave Millie and Isla a dark look.

"We better watch it," Isla whispered under her breath. "Her highness is giving us the look."

The women grew quiet, respectfully listening to Sophia's port talk. To her credit, she gave Siren of the Seas ship and its crewmembers glowing praise before discussing the first stop at Guernsey and Saint Peter Port, the second largest of the Channel Islands.

She finished touching on the highlights, and even Millie was wishing she could visit Guernsey and the ancient Castle Cornet, which had guarded the harbor for eight hundred years. Sophia ended her presentation, and several passengers lingered to ask questions.

"Time to get to work." Isla snatched a pile of pamphlets off the nearby table and began handing them to the people exiting the gallery.

Finally, the room cleared until only Millie, Sophia and Isla remained. Sophia finished putting away her supplies and met them near the exit.

"It was a wonderful presentation," Millie said graciously. "It made me want to get off and explore Guernsey as well."

"Of course, my presentation was top notch. That's why Andrew hired me." She shot Millie an annoyed look and turned to Isla. "Andrew said you'll be heading ashore to explore the port area."

"I am. Millie is going to go with me."

Sophia pinned Millie with an imperious look. "Don't you ever work?"

Millie refused to take the bait. "Of course. In fact, I'm working right now, and Andy should be giving me combat pay."

"What's that supposed to mean?" Sophia snapped.

"It means whatever you think it does." Millie refused to spend another second with the troublesome woman.

She motioned to Isla. "I'll see you at six." Without a backward glance, Millie strode out of the gallery, all the while mentally berating Andy for hiring the annoying woman.

By the time she reached her next activity, a pub quiz, aka trivia, in the Marseille Lounge, Millie had calmed. During the quiz, she learned even more about the first port stop and Victor Hugo, the novelist who wrote Les Misérables. He lived in Hauteville House on Guernsey for more than a decade, where he published the novel in 1862. Les Misérables, one of the longest novels ever written, was a whopping 1,900 pages.

Up next was an Irish step dance lesson with one of the new Celtic performers. Millie was thankful the lesson lasted only half an hour as the tips of her toes, her calves and her hips began to ache.

It wasn't until Millie limped off the stage to go change before meeting Isla in the atrium that an actual plan began to form in her mind...the perfect plan to try to track down Sharky's kidnappers and hopefully rescue him before it was too late.

Chapter 22

"Are you sure about this?" Isla wrinkled her nose as she consulted the printout Millie had brought with her, the street map of the area and legend of the hostels; one of which she suspected was where Sharky was being held against his will.

"I'm not sure about anything," Millie admitted. "My gut tells me Sharky is somewhere in this area based on his notes, comments by the bartender and Halbert, not to mention the location of the ransom demand. The proximity is perfect for someone to snatch up the cash, make a dash for the ferry and be out of the country before the authorities even start looking."

"It's a solid plan," Isla admitted. "I mean, if I were going to kidnap the owner of a mega cruise line and demand a ransom, this would probably work best."

"These kidnappers have no plans to release Sharky since he can ID them, at least identify Svetlana, which means somewhere along the line they plan to kill him. He's too much of a potential liability."

The women turned the corner and approached a brick building, which reminded Millie of a city brownstone. They climbed the steps and entered a narrow hall. The overpowering aroma of bleach combined with a lemony citrus burned her nose. "Good grief."

Isla blinked rapidly as she made a choking sound. "The smell is lethal. It's burning my lungs."

"Cover your mouth."

Isla flung her arm across her mouth. "Which way?" she asked in a muffled voice.

"I guess we'll start down here." They made their way to the end of the hall, and a door marked, "Manager."

Millie gave it a sharp rap. No one answered, so she tried again. "No one's answering. On to Plan B." The women retraced their steps and climbed the stairs to the second floor.

"Hang on." Millie pulled a thin, gold key from her jacket pocket.

"You have a key to this place?"

"No. It's a key I found in my junk drawer. I have no idea what it's for." She tightened her grip. "Here goes nothing."

They stopped when they reached the first door with a bronze-colored number four on the front. She inserted the key and began twisting it back and forth, all the while lightly thumping on the exterior.

The door flew open, and a man in a white t-shirt, his hair slicked back, glared at them. "What do you want?"

"We rented a room. I'm looking for unit three."

"This is number four." The man motioned to the number four on the front. "Can't you read?"

"Whoops. Sorry."

"Stupid Americans." The man slammed the door in Millie's face.

Isla's eyes grew wide. "That went well."

Millie shrugged. "On to the next one."

"How many rental rooms are in this building?"

"Four, and there are four hostels in our targeted area." Millie approached the next door, repeating the same steps. No one answered, so she began rapping loudly. There was still no answer. She bent down to peer into the keyhole.

"What are you doing?" Isla hissed.

"Trying to sneak a peek inside. These old buildings aren't as airtight as the newer, more modern buildings."

"Can you see anything?"

Millie closed her left eye and squinted her right eye as she attempted to see through the hole. "Not much. Just some flowery wallpaper, something similar to what my grandmother had on her walls."

They stepped to the next door, repeating the key in lock trick. The door opened, and a young woman holding a small child answered. "Hey."

"Sorry." Millie apologized as she waved the key. "Wrong room."

The door closed and the women approached the final rental unit. An elderly woman answered and then slammed the door in their faces.

"What a friendly bunch," Isla joked. "Isn't she a little old to be staying in a hostel?"

"I guess there aren't any age restrictions. At least we can tick one hostel off our list." The women trudged down the steps, stopping when they reached the sidewalk. "This building was a bust."

Millie led the way to the end of the sidewalk, and they turned the corner. The street was busier than the previous street. On the opposite side was a river. She pointed to a sign. "Can you read that?"

"Yeah." Isla nodded. "It's the River Itchen. It's pretty, at least from what I can see of it."

"It is pretty," Millie agreed. "A pretty good spot to dump a body." She started walking, and Isla fell into step. "Maybe they won't kill Sharky. Maybe they'll leave him behind to be found after they're long gone."

"It's possible, but I doubt it." Millie slowed when they reached the next hostel. "This is it." She tried the front door. The door was locked. "We can't get in."

"There's a notice." Isla pointed to a sheet of paper taped to one of the windows.

Millie bounced on her tiptoes as she leaned over the railing. "It's a non-compliance notice of some sort. This place isn't even open." She stepped close to the front door, pressing her forehead to the pane as she peered through the etched glass.

The hallways and stairs were littered with boxes and debris. There were no signs of life. "I guess we can scratch this one off our list."

The street dead-ended, and Millie and Isla backtracked, past the empty building and the first hostel they'd investigated. They walked another block and turned onto a narrow cobblestone alley.

Isla slowed. "This place is creepy. I don't think we're at the right place."

Millie consulted her map. "Nope. This is it." She took a hesitant step forward. "Somewhere around here are six hostel units."

"I would never stay here," Isla said in a low voice.

"Me either. Unless I was kidnapping someone and holding them for ransom." Millie's scalp began to tingle, and she got the eerie sensation they were being watched. She forced the thought from her mind and focused on Sharky instead.

He needed them...needed their help.

Millie climbed the steps, grasped the handle of the thick wooden door and pushed it open. The hinges let out a high-pitched squeal that echoed in the hall. A man stepped out of a door marked "office," a scowl on his face.

"Whatcha be doin' around here?"

Millie tightened her grip on the key she was still holding. The plan to try the doors of the hostel units flew right out the window. She frantically racked her brain for an excuse. "You're the manager?"

"I am."

"We...we're looking for a friend. He has black hair, about this tall and kind of roundish."

"Don't have anyone staying here who matches that description."

Millie fumbled inside her pocket and pulled out her cell phone. She showed the man the picture of Sharky. "This is him."

The man frowned as he glanced at the screen. "Never seen him before in my life."

"You're sure?"

"Are you hard of hearing? That's what I said."

Isla grasped Millie's arm. "He's not here. Let's keep looking." She began backing down the hall.

"Thank you for your time."

The man grunted, and Millie hurriedly followed Isla out of the building. "There are some rude people around here."

"It's not the best of areas." Isla swallowed hard. "I can't shake the feeling we're being watched."

"I'm getting the same vibe. We better get a move on." Millie didn't let her guard down until they reached the sidewalk.

"If my calculations are correct, we're down to one building and two rentals," Isla said.

"We are, and these two units are our most promising prospects. The hostel is in the perfect location and kind of off the beaten path."

"Even more off the beaten path than the place we just left?"

"Good point. I noticed on the hostel calendar this one has a vacancy starting tomorrow, which would fit into Sharky's kidnapper's schedule if they plan to skip town after grabbing the ransom money," Millie said. "Not to mention they accept cash, and the rental rate is twenty pounds per night, which is the exact amount Sharky mentioned in his journal."

Isla shook her head. "I don't know how you keep up with all of the clues. I never would've thought about that."

"It takes years of practice," Millie grinned. Her smile quickly faded. "This is it. We either find Sharky here or I'm out of ideas."

The burnt orange building was tall and thin. It reminded Millie of a mini castle, complete with turrets. They entered through the open gate and stepped onto a sidewalk leading to the front entrance. A black wrought iron fence lined both sides.

The women climbed the steps where two concrete gargoyles stood sentinel, watching their every move.

"Gargoyles." Isla reached out to touch one. "This place is right out of a slasher horror movie."

"It's unique. I'll give you that." Millie eased the door open and stepped into a large reception area. The walls were a crimson color. Floor-to-ceiling windows faced the street.

Dim streaks of light beamed in through the thick cobalt blue drapes covering both windows. The wooden floor creaked as they made their way to a reception desk on the left. There was a small silver bell on top of the desk.

Isla gave it a light tap. *Ding*.

The curtained doorway fluttered, and an elderly man emerged. "Can I help you?"

"I hope so. We're looking for a hostel for a friend, and saw you have a room available starting tomorrow."

"I do." The man studied them through his wire-rimmed glasses. "It's twenty pounds a night. The room shares a bath with two other guest rooms. Minimum stay is three nights."

"So it's sixty pounds for three nights," Millie verified.

"Sixty pounds, but it won't be available until tomorrow afternoon."

"I don't suppose there's a chance we could take a look at the room," Millie said hopefully.

"Let me check." The man lowered his gaze, peering at something behind the counter. "I'm sorry. That won't be possible. The unit is occupied by the current tenant." He pointed to a binder next to the silver bell. "I have pictures of the unit if you would like to take a look."

"I would." Millie eagerly reached for the binder and flipped it open.

"It's unit number two in the back."

Isla and Millie leaned in, studying the pictures. "This unit has two bunk beds."

"Two beds and a rollaway if you need it, but I'll have to charge you an extra ten pounds if more than two people are occupying the room...cost of water and utilities and all."

"I see," Millie murmured. "You said this unit is in the back. Is it on the ground floor?"

"Yes. Ground floor. All of my rental rooms are in the back."

"And your other room is still occupied?"

"It is. Do you need more than one room? I thought you said it was for a friend."

"I...I'm only looking for one. I want to know what's available so I can pass it on. Can I take your number in case he wants the room?"

"My number is on my card." The man placed a business card on the counter, and Millie picked it up. "Thank you." She turned to go and then hesitated. He seemed like such a nice, old man. "I also have a friend who's gone missing. I wonder if perhaps you've seen him."

Millie removed her cell phone from her pocket and showed Sharky's picture to him. He studied the picture and then slowly shook his head. "No. I've never seen him before."

"Thank you." Millie gave him a sad smile, realizing she had finally hit a dead end. She couldn't see the room, couldn't get past the innkeeper to scope them out.

The women made their way to the door when the man spoke. "Not sure if your friend is looking for a place with parking. Unlike some of the other rentals in the area, we have parking in the alley out back."

"I'll let him know." Millie thanked the old man again and made her way out of the building and onto the sidewalk.

"I'm sorry, Millie. You tried," Isla said. "I just thought of something. I thought there were only two rental rooms here."

"There are." Millie consulted her notes. "Two rooms for rent."

"But the man said you would be sharing the bathroom with two other rentals."

"You're right. He did." Millie tapped her chin thoughtfully and took several steps to the side, peering down the walkway separating the rental property and the building next to it. "He mentioned a parking area in the alley in the back. Since we're already here, I say we go have a look."

She began walking along the side, past the iron fence.

"I don't think..." Isla ran after her. "What if the old man wants to know what we're doing?"

"We tell him we decided to check out the parking arrangements before we left."

The women reached the back of the building which spilled into an alley. There was a row of brick buildings on the opposite side.

Millie wandered to the center of the alley and pivoted, turning her attention to the back of the hostel. "He said the available unit was in the back and on the ground floor."

"All of the units are in the back."

The window blinds were closed, making it impossible for Millie to sneak a peek inside. She crept toward one of the windows.

"What are you doing?" Isla asked.

Millie motioned for her to be quiet, continuing to make her way to the window. She stepped closer until she was eye level with the lower windowsill. "Sharky...where are you?" She pressed a light hand to the pane, willing him to give her some sign he was there.

The units were the perfect spot to hide someone. The renter could pay in cash, sneak someone in and out through the back alley and the owner would never know. But there was no way to find out if Millie's hunch was right. She said a small prayer for Sharky before reluctantly removing her hand.

"C'mon, Millie. You did everything humanly possible, short of busting down the doors." Isla began gently leading her away from the building and down the alley.

"Isla, you're a genius." Millie pulled her arm back. "What time is it?"

Isla glanced at her watch. "We have an hour left before we have to be back on board the ship."

"You gave me a great idea. The owner said the unit...the one that's going to be available tomorrow - that someone is in there. They were occupied."

"Right," Isla agreed. "Which means he's able to track the tenants via an electronic entry system."

"So, if Svetlana is occupying one of these units, she's here."

"Correct again, but we can't wait all day for her to make an appearance."

"We won't have to." Millie's eyes traveled up the side of the building and the fire escape, which ran along the wall. "This might be a desperate move, but I think I found a way to flush everyone out of the building."

Chapter 23

"What are you going to do?" Isla asked.

"*We*. What are *we* going to do?" Millie jabbed her finger at the fire escape. "If this building is anything like the ones in the States, they're required to have fire alarms."

"I suppose."

"All I need to do is find the common area's fire alarm and set it off, forcing everyone to evacuate the building."

"Including Svetlana."

"Bingo. And since the units are here in the back, whoever is in the building will most likely exit through this door."

"But how are you going to get to Sharky?"

"That's where my plan gets a little tricky." Millie began to pace.

"One of us pulls the alarm. While everyone is running out, the other one runs into the unit to check it out. I hate to be the 'suggester' of bad news, but what if they already got rid of Sharky?" Isla said. "And he's not here."

"Donovan and Patterson think Sharky is still alive. His kidnappers will wait until the last minute to take him out in case they have to prove he's still alive to collect the ransom. They planned to reveal the location of where to drop the ransom money in an email tomorrow."

Isla followed Millie's gaze, studying the back of the building. "I'll pull the alarm, and you run inside."

"First, we have to locate it." Millie eased the back door open and Isla followed close behind. The women inched forward, careful to stay close to the sides of the hall. They reached the end and then tiptoed back to their starting point.

Millie stepped out of the building and waited for Isla to join her. "I didn't see an alarm."

"It was there," Isla said. "Near the exit. It's a bright red box on the left-hand side."

"Seriously?" Millie eased the door open and stuck her head inside. She slipped back out. "How did I miss that?"

"It's in the perfect spot. I can pull the alarm and run for cover," Isla said.

"It's a great plan, but something is missing." Millie studied the building's exterior. "We need backup. If Sharky is here, once Svetlana and her accomplice realize we're onto them, they might attack us. The old man isn't going to be much help."

"We could call in a suspicious person to the authorities," Isla suggested. "What's the emergency code to get help?"

"It's an idea, but even if we got the authorities over here, they're not going to search each of the units without probable cause. I would rather call

Patterson. He's around here somewhere." Millie slipped her cell phone from her pocket. She scrolled her contacts list until she located Patterson's cell phone number. Millie pressed send. "Here goes nothing."

"Dave Patterson speaking."

"Patterson, it's Millie."

"Hey, Millie."

"There's a slim chance we tracked down Svetlana and maybe even Sharky."

"How..." Patterson let out a heavy sigh. "Never mind. Where are you?"

"Not far from River Itchen." Millie rattled off the address. "I'm standing in the back alley, getting ready to flush them out."

"Flush them out?"

"I have an idea but figured it would probably be wise to have some backup. The building owner is in no condition to come to my aid if my hunch is correct."

"You should stay out of this, Millie," Patterson warned.

"I can't. Have you found Sharky?"

There was silence on the other end.

"We're running out of time. I think I'm onto something."

"Stay put. I'm on my way." Patterson ended the call, not giving Millie a chance to say good-bye.

"He's on the way, but I don't think he's very happy. I'm envisioning a major lecture in my future."

"Mine too," Isla said glumly.

"You can take off, and he'll never know you were part of this."

"And miss all of the action?" Isla joked. "We're a team. We're in this together."

"I'll make sure he knows you had no idea what you were getting yourself into until it was too late."

It was a long ten minutes before Dave Patterson, accompanied by three of the ship's security personnel, turned the corner and strode down the back alley. "Well?"

"We're waiting on you," Millie said. "We think Sharky is being held captive inside this building."

"I'm surprised to see you here, Isla."

"This was all my idea. I dragged Isla along."

"I can believe it." Patterson crossed his arms. "How exactly do you intend to flush out the building's occupants?"

"By pulling the fire alarm near the rear entrance," Millie said.

"What if they're not in there?"

"We spoke to the owner, inquiring about a room. He told us he would have given us a look around the room, but the renters were on-premise, so he couldn't let us in."

"What makes you think Svetlana and possibly even Sharky are here?"

"Process of elimination. Sharky mentioned the river. He mentioned a hostel. His ATM card was used two blocks from here. He met with Svetlana at a dive bar around the corner. Isla and I checked every hostel rental unit in the vicinity."

"How did you do that?" Patterson briefly closed his eyes. "Never mind. I'm sure I don't want to know."

"This hostel unit is the most promising. According to the online calendar and the manager we spoke with, the lower right-hand unit is available starting tomorrow for a price that matches the one Sharky noted in his journal. It's the unit where I think the kidnappers are holding him."

"Journal?" Patterson interrupted.

"We can discuss it later," Millie said. "I think you're right. Svetlana and her partner are keeping Sharky alive until the last minute. First thing tomorrow, they're going to get rid of him on the way to pick up the ransom money. Once they have what they hope is the money, they plan to hop on the ferry that will take them out of the country."

"There is a ferry that travels to another port and then on to France departing late morning," Patterson confirmed.

"Which means Svetlana and her partner plan to be on it with a boatload of cash."

"Boatload?" Patterson smiled. "What if you pull the smoke alarm, the building clears, we run in and look for Sharky and he's not here?"

"Then I give up," Millie said.

Patterson pressed a hand to her forehead. "Are you feeling all right?"

Millie swatted it away. "I'm all out of ideas."

"That's a first."

Millie ignored the jab. "So, are you going to hang around and see what happens?"

Patterson pressed the tips of his fingers together as he stared at Millie.

"Plan B would be to march inside and knock on the door. All they'll have to do is refuse to let you in, and then you've tipped them off that we're onto them, sealing Sharky's fate if he's here."

"Your plan could easily blow up in our faces," Patterson argued.

"Yes, it could, and it wouldn't be the first time. Unfortunately, it's all I have, unless you have a better idea."

"I'm fresh out. Against my better judgment, I'm going to agree to your plan." Patterson motioned to his men. "Let's get out of sight." He tapped Millie's arm. "Since this was your idea, you get the honors."

Chapter 24

At Patterson's direction, two of the ship's security guards made their way around the front of the building and moved into position.

Once they were in position, Patterson and the other guard, along with Isla, eased in between two buildings, catty-corner to the rear entrance of the hostel. The location offered a partial view of the back of the building and an unobstructed view of the rear entrance.

"Here goes nothing." Millie held her breath as she darted up the steps. She flung the door open and swung to the side. With a sharp intake of breath, she braced herself before grasping hold of the fire alarm's handle and pulling hard.

Millie ran out of the door and bolted down the steps. She was halfway across the alley when it dawned on her nothing had happened.

Patterson stepped out of his hiding spot and shook his head.

Millie lifted her hands and shrugged. She returned to the doorway, eased it open and craned her neck. The handle was only partially engaged. "Second time is the charm." She gritted her teeth and pressed hard on the handle.

A shrill, shrieking wail pierced the air. Millie ran down the steps and dove behind nearby trashcans.

The hostel's back door flew open. Several of the occupants scrambled out of the building and ran into the alleyway.

One was a young couple with a small child. Following close behind was a middle-aged man wearing a ball cap and clutching a briefcase. A second man, this one taller and younger, ran out after them.

Bringing up the rear was a woman, her hair pulled back in a ponytail. Millie squinted her eyes, and her heart started to race. The hairstyle was different, but despite the change in appearance, she was certain it was Svetlana. The pony-tailed woman was wearing a pair of jeans, a t-shirt and carrying a backpack.

Svetlana joined the younger man. They stood off to the side, talking in low voices. Millie emerged from her hiding spot and marched across the alley. "Where is he?"

Svetlana gave Millie an irritated look before her eyes widened, and she knew the woman recognized her. "Vut are you talking a-bout?"

"Svetlana," Millie spat out her name. "Where is Sharky?"

"I have no idea vut you are talking about," she repeated. "You must have me mistaken for someone else."

"No. I don't."

Millie caught a glimpse of Patterson as he crept behind the occupants and made his way inside the building. She needed to keep the couple distracted until he could get inside the rental unit. "You catfished Sharky and conned him out of money. He somehow convinced you that he was president of a cruise ship line, so you decided it was worth your time to meet him here. Once you lured him to your meeting place, you drugged him. Somewhere along the line, you decided to kidnap him and hold him for ransom."

"You...you're crazy." The woman began speaking in another language before switching back to broken English. "I'm calling the authorities."

"Calling the authorities is an excellent idea. I'm sure they'll be interested in checking your room and belongings."

The old man Millie met earlier stumbled out the back door. "Is everyone all right? It was a false alarm."

"It vuz her fault." Svetlana gave Millie a shove. "She is stalking me. I vont to press charges."

Millie could feel a hot rage fill her, and she shoved the woman back. "Do it," she taunted. "Call the authorities."

"I am not going to put up vid dis." Svetlana swept past Millie, and she and the man began walking toward the building. They made it as far as the back door when two of the ship's security guards burst out of the rear exit.

"That's them!" Millie shouted.

The security guards circled the couple.

"What is going on here?" the owner shouted.

The faint sounds of sirens grew louder. Moments later, police vehicles careened around the corner and into the alley.

Millie ran past the residents. She raced into the building, and to the room she suspected was

Svetlana's. Patterson was inside, kneeling next to a pale Sharky who was sprawled out on the floor.

"Is he..." Millie couldn't get the words out. Sharky was still...almost too still.

"He's alive. It appears he's heavily sedated," Patterson pressed a light hand to Sharky's wrist. "An ambulance is en route."

The local authorities burst into the room, followed by men in medical uniforms. Patterson backed away and guided Millie off to the side.

"Please, God." Millie prayed as she watched the emergency workers assess Sharky's situation. They made quick work of hooking him up to several pieces of equipment, including an IV, and then they loaded him onto a stretcher.

Patterson joined the uniformed men while Millie followed Sharky and the rescue workers out of the building. She watched as they placed him inside the back of the emergency vehicle and drove off.

"Millie." There was a light hand on her shoulder. It was Isla. "I heard the authorities talking a minute ago. They said he's going to be okay. Sharky is going to be okay."

Sudden tears burned the back of her eyes, and her lower lip began to tremble. "Thank God. I..." She stumbled to the stoop and sank down on a step.

Isla joined her. "You saved Sharky's life."

The crowd grew as two uniformed men placed Svetlana and her partner in the back of one of the patrol cars. Several local authorities made their rounds talking to the residents. One of them approached Millie and Isla.

The women repeated all that had happened from the moment they entered the hostel and spoke with the owner. While they were telling their story, one of the officials climbed into the vehicle containing Svetlana and her partner and drove off.

Millie finished answering the questions and phoned Andy to fill him in on what had happened.

She assured him that she and Isla would return as soon as the authorities released them.

Dusk was settling in by the time they finally finished searching the building and loading bags of what Millie believed was potential evidence into their vehicles.

The last officer, the one Millie guessed was the lead investigator, finally climbed into his car and drove off. Patterson and his men joined Millie and Isla. "You're not gonna believe this."

"Svetlana isn't her real name."

"It's her real name," Patterson said. "Svetlana Orlov, to be exact. She's wanted in Ukraine for embezzlement, armed robbery and impersonating an intelligence agent. Her partner, Barlis Kremlev, isn't much better."

"So, she wasn't who Sharky thought she was."

"Not by a long shot." Patterson extended his hands and helped both women to their feet. "I take it you told Andy you were running late."

"I did."

"It's time to head home." Patterson began walking down the alley. Millie and Isla joined him while his men followed behind. "I have some good news."

"Sharky is going to be okay. Isla overheard a couple of the men talking."

"He is. I just got an update. Not only okay, but he's alive and kicking and throwing a hissy fit. As soon as they hooked him up and began flushing the bad stuff out of his system, he started to come around. I think the hospital is going to kick him out and send him back to us in time for him to join the ship before we leave port tomorrow."

"That is good news." Millie clapped her hands. "I'm ready to have the old Sharky back."

Patterson grinned. "I have more good news. There's a reward for the capture of Svetlana and Barlis."

Millie slowed. "A reward?"

"Fifty thousand rubles."

"Fifty thousand rubles."

"It's about seven hundred and fifty bucks."

"Hey. It's free money." Millie's cell phone started to chime. It was Nic. "Hello."

"Hey, Millie. Where are you?"

"On my way back to the ship with Patterson, Isla and the security guys. I'm sure you heard."

"Heard? It's all anyone on board is talking about. Am I going to have to put a tracker on you?" her husband joked.

"That might not be a bad idea."

"I'm glad you're safe, and that you called Patterson to cover your back. He's impressed."

"Patterson is impressed? That's a first." Millie shot the chief of security a wide grin. "Not only is Sharky going to be okay, but I'm in line for a reward for Svetlana and her partner's apprehension. Fifty thousand rubles."

"So, you're treating me to dinner?" Nic teased.

"Any time you want."

Andy, Donovan and Nic, along with several of the other security personnel met them at the ship. It was almost a ticker-tape parade a la cruise ship.

Millie beamed as they crossed to the other side of the atrium.

"Millie saves the day," Donovan proclaimed.

"I had some help." Millie tapped Patterson's arm. "Patterson and Isla were my wingmen. I couldn't have done it without either of them...without any of them."

Millie, Patterson and Isla briefly told them what had happened, and after the crowd dispersed, Millie ran up to the apartment to switch into her uniform to start her shift.

She flew through her evening schedule, thrilled to be doing what she loved even more than snooping...entertaining the passengers.

It was almost midnight before she finished her hosting events and headed home. Nic was already there and ready for bed. She joined him a short time later, and they both prayed for Sharky's recovery.

Nic quickly drifted off to sleep, but Millie lay awake for a long time going over the events of the week, how they had almost lost Sharky, and she thanked God she was able to track him down.

Before she fell asleep, Millie remembered there was one more thing she wanted to do before the ship left port, something important.

Chapter 25

Millie was awake early before the alarm went off. She sprang from the bed and headed to the shower. She made quick work of getting ready and found Nic downstairs making coffee. "You're chipper this morning."

"I am. It's going to be a great day."

"Yes, it is. We're finally going to be on our way." Nic gave his wife a quick kiss and then ran upstairs to get ready. When he returned a short time later, he grabbed a bran muffin and a thermos filled with coffee before heading out.

Millie wasn't far behind him. Her first stop was the galley, remembering her promise to Annette the evening before, to swing by and pick her up before running their very important errand.

Annette was already waiting. She grabbed two large bags that were sitting on the counter. "Are you ready?"

"I am." Millie nodded toward the bags of food. "Is security going to let us off the ship? I thought taking food items off was a no-no."

"It is, but we purchased these items in port. There are no foreign plants or potential cross-contamination. It will be fine."

"You would know. Let's go."

The women made their way down the stairs to the crewmember's gangway, dinging their cards as they passed through the security checkpoint. They reached the end of the dock and turned left.

"I hope Halbert is still around," Millie said breathlessly as she struggled to keep up with Annette's quick pace.

"He lives here. I'm sure he's nearby."

The women slowed as they approached the dark warehouse.

"Halbert?" Millie called out. "Are you here?"

There was a thudding noise coming from inside. A bleary-eyed Halbert Pennyman appeared in the doorway.

"Did we wake you?"

"It's okay. I was thinkin' about getting up." Halbert lifted his hands over his head and stretched. "What brings you here this early?"

"We'll be leaving soon." Annette stepped forward. "These are for you." She held out the bags of food.

"For me?" Halbert brightened.

"It's non-perishable foods. There's some granola, cans of nuts, some bottled water, dried meats and canned fruit."

"I...thank you." His hand trembled as he took the bags from Annette.

"And I have something for you too." Millie handed him the bag of clothes she'd gathered from Nic's closet, with his permission. "I think you'll find a few items and some shoes that will fit nicely."

Halbert peered into the bag, his eyes shining brightly. "You are too kind."

Millie swallowed hard, fighting the urge to break down. "And you are a good man, Halbert Pennyman."

Halbert set the bags of food and clothing on the worn workbench. "You're going to be back here next week?"

"Yes," Millie nodded. "We'll be back every twelve days to drop off passengers and pick up new ones."

"Then maybe I'll see you again?" Halbert asked hopefully.

Millie lightly touched the man's arm. "I'm sure you'll see us again, Halbert. You take care of yourself, okay?"

The women made their way home to Siren of the Seas. Back on board, Millie was the first to speak. "It's sad."

"Yes," Annette agreed. "At least now he knows someone cares."

"Nic told me that Sharky returned to the ship late last night. I was thinking about stopping by to check on him."

"He had better count his blessings that Millie Armati didn't give up on finding him."

"And Patterson," Millie added.

"And Patterson." Annette headed upstairs to the galley while Millie ran down to the maintenance office. There was no sign of Sharky, but Reef was inside.

He did a double take when he saw Millie. "Hey, there's the ship's hero."

"Is Sharky around?"

"He's coming in later. He's still kinda groggy from the drugs. I know he's awake, though. Why don't you run by his place? He's anxious to talk to you."

"I think I will." Millie slipped out of the office and made the quick trip to Sharky's cabin. The door was ajar, and she knocked lightly.

"It's open."

Millie stuck her head around the corner and found a pale Sharky lying in the lower bunk. "Millie. Come in."

She tiptoed into the cramped space.

"Have a seat."

She scooched around Sharky's scooter and pulled out the desk chair, perching on the edge. "How are you feeling?"

"I'm feeling like I'm lucky to be alive." Sharky struggled to a sitting position. "I owe you an apology. I'm sorry I accused you of stalking me and for reporting you to Donovan."

"It's okay. I understand. I mean, if I were in your shoes, I might have done the same thing."

"You saved my life. Patterson told me you refused to give up. You kept looking for me."

Millie lowered her gaze and stared at her clasped hands. "My gut told me you were in trouble."

"You ain't kidding on that one. At first, Svetlana and I hit it off. She took me to her rented room, and that's when it started."

"When what started?"

Sharky told Millie that Svetlana was hinting she didn't have enough money to pay for her hostel, so he gave her some cash. He admitted to Millie he'd fibbed to Svetlana and even gone as far as to have business cards printed to impress the woman. "Little did I know I was setting myself up to be kidnapped."

"You had no idea." Millie had another thought. "Patterson said your debit card was used at a local ATM."

"That's another story. I was starting to get a little suspicious after giving her cash to pay for her room rental. We went out for dinner. When we came back to her room for a little romantic time, he was there."

"Barlis," Millie guessed.

"Yeah. That's when the fun began. By then, I was feelin' woozy. I think she slipped something into my drink. Next thing I know, I'm tied up on the floor, and her and her buddy are talkin' in some foreign language." Sharky told Millie they let the drug wear off and then escorted him to a nearby ATM where they forced him to withdraw cash.

"So Patterson *was* right. It was you the store clerk saw using the ATM."

"It was. As soon as we got back to the room, they drugged me again. I pretended to be out before it kicked in. I heard them talking about the ransom note, their plan to collect the cash and flee the country on the ferry."

"Right here at the port."

"Yeah. Reef said they attacked Nikki and a homeless man, too."

"I believe they were responsible. They were scoping out the area for the money drop. Nikki and Halbert, the homeless man, happened to be in the wrong place at the wrong time."

"Right." Sharky's eyelids started to droop, and Millie stood.

"I'm going to let you get some rest."

"I'll see you later, Millie. I owe you one."

"You don't owe me anything. That's what friends are for. I'm just glad that you're okay."

Sharky's eyes fluttered and then closed. He muttered something, and Millie could've sworn he repeated her words, "That's what friends are for."

The end.

*If you enjoyed reading "Southampton Stalker,"
please take a moment to leave a review. It would mean
so much to me. Thank you! -Hope Callaghan*

**The series continues...Cruise Ship Cozy
Mysteries Book 18 Coming Soon!**

Books in This Series

Reindeer & Robberies: Book 15
Transatlantic Tragedy: Book 16
Southampton Stalker: Book 17
Book 18: Coming Soon!
Cruise Ship Cozy Mysteries Box Set I (Books 1-3)
Cruise Ship Cozy Mysteries Box Set II (Books 4-6)
Cruise Ship Cozy Mysteries Box Set III (Books 7-9)
Cruise Ship Cozy Mysteries Box Set IV (Books 10-12)
Cozy Mysteries 12 Book Box Set: (Garden Girls &
Cruise Ship Series)

Get New Releases & More

Get New Releases, Giveaways & Discounted eBooks When You Subscribe To My Free Cozy Mysteries Newsletter!

hopecallaghan.com/newsletter

Meet Author Hope Callaghan

Hope loves to connect with her readers! Connect with her today!

Facebook: authorhopecallaghan

Amazon: Hope Callaghan

Pinterest: cozymysteriesauthor

Never miss another book deal! Text the word Books to 33222

Visit **hopecallaghan.com/newsletter** for special offers, free books, and soon-to-be-released books!

Hope Callaghan is an American author who loves to write clean fiction books, especially Christian Mystery and Cozy Mystery books. She has written more than 70 mystery books (and counting) in six series.

In March 2017, Hope won a Mom's Choice Award for her book, "Key to Savannah," Book 1 in the Made in Savannah Cozy Mystery Series.

Born and raised in a small town in West Michigan, she now lives in Florida with her husband.

She is the proud mother of 3 children. When she's not doing the thing she loves best - writing books - she enjoys cooking, traveling and reading books.

Caramel Apple Mini Cheesecakes Recipe

Ingredients:

Graham/Oats Crust:

¼ cup brown sugar

1 cup graham cracker crumbs

¾ cup rolled oats

½ cup melted butter

Cheesecake:

2 – 8 oz packages softened cream cheese

2 tbsp corn starch

¼ cup brown sugar

¼ cup white sugar

1/2 tsp ginger

2 tsp vanilla extract

1 tsp cinnamon

Streusel / Apple Crisp Topping:

¼ cup all-purpose flour

¼ cup rolled oats

¼ cup brown sugar

½ tsp cinnamon

A "pinch" of nutmeg (1/8 tsp.)

2-3 tbsp coconut oil

1/8 cup chopped walnut (optional)

1 large apple, peeled cored and finely chopped (I used ambrosia gold)

Caramel Topping, if desired. (I used Simply Concord Caramel Dip.)

Directions:

-Preheat oven to 350 degrees.

-In a medium size mixing bowl combine graham cracker crumbs, rolled oats, melted butter and brown sugar.

-Line 16-18 muffin cups with liners.

-Press roughly one tablespoon of crust mixture inside the bottom of each muffin cup.

-Bake for 5 minutes. Remove from oven. Let cool.

-While crust cools, use an electric mixer to blend together cream cheese, brown sugar, white sugar, cinnamon, ginger, cornstarch and vanilla.

-Scoop cheesecake mixture on top of your mini

graham cracker/oat crusts, leaving room at the top for fruit and streusel topping.

-Combine all streusel ingredients (except for the apple slices). Mix together until crumbly.

-Add single layer of finely chopped apple to the top of the cheesecake.

-Cover the apple with a LIGHT layer of the Apple Crisp Topping.

-Bake at 350F for 25-30 minutes. Remove from oven.

-Let cool for at least 15 minutes. Cover and refrigerate overnight.

-Top with caramel sauce and serve.

Makes 16-18 cheesecakes.

Printed in Great Britain
by Amazon